PENGUIN MODERN CLASSICS
Boyhood

BHISHAM SAHNI (1915–2003) was an iconic writer who transformed the landscape of Hindi literature. Sahni was fluent in several languages—Punjabi, Hindi, Sanskrit, Urdu and English—and his oeuvre encompassed a wide range of literary forms: novels, short stories, plays, essays. *Tamas*, his best-known novel, won the Sahitya Akademi Award in 1975 and was subsequently adapted into a National Award–winning film by Govind Nihalani. His other well-known novels include, among others, *Jharokhe* (published in Penguin Classics as *Boyhood*), *Basanti* and *Mayyadas Ki Marhi* (published in Penguin Classics as *Mansion*). Sahni also wrote numerous short stories (a selection of which has been published in Penguin Classics as *Middle India*), six plays and a biography of his brother, the eminent film and stage actor Balraj Sahni. His autobiography, *Aaj Ke Ateet*, is published in Penguin Classics as *Today's Pasts*.

Born in Rawalpindi, Sahni later went to college in Lahore. In his youth he became involved with the Indian People's Theatre Association as well as the Indian National Congress. After Partition, he settled down in Delhi and began to teach at Delhi University. From 1957–63, he was in the USSR to work as a translator at the Foreign Languages Publishing House, before returning to Delhi. He edited the literary journal *Nayi Kahaniyan* from 1965–67, and was the general secretary of the All-India Progressive Writers' Association from 1975–85.

Sahni was awarded the Padma Bhushan in 1998, and the Shalaka Samman, the Delhi government's highest literary prize, in 1999.

ANNA KHANNA completed her master's from Glasgow University in French and German literature and language with additional subjects in the fine arts. On coming to India, she taught both French and English literature and language at the British School in Delhi, where she became deputy headmistress. She also taught at the American School, Alliance Francaise and at Lucknow University.

Her book reviews and articles on design and culture have been published in leading newspapers. Prior to her English translation of the novel *Jharokhe* (published in Penguin Classics as *Boyhood*), done in consultation with the author, she had translated and published a number of short stories by Bhisham Sahni.

BY THE SAME AUTHOR

Tamas
Today's Pasts
Basanti
Mansion

BHISHAM SAHNI

Boyhood

Translated from the Hindi by Anna Khanna

PENGUIN BOOKS

An imprint of Penguin Random House

PENGUIN BOOKS

USA | Canada | UK | Ireland | Australia
New Zealand | India | South Africa | China | Singapore

Penguin Books is part of the Penguin Random House group of companies
whose addresses can be found at global.penguinrandomhouse.com

Published by Penguin Random House India Pvt. Ltd
4th Floor, Capital Tower 1, MG Road,
Gurugram 122 002, Haryana, India

First published in Hindi as *Jharokhe* by Rajkamal Prakashan 1967
First published by Penguin Books India 2016

ISBN 9780143420071

Typeset in Adobe Caslon Pro by Manipal Digital Systems, Manipal
Printed at Manipal Technologies Limited, India

www.penguin.co.in

This is a legitimate digitally printed version of the book and therefore might not
have certain extra finishing on the cover.

To Kalpana

Sometimes, fragmented images of the past which have fallen into the dark abyss of oblivion, begin to fly around like so many scraps of paper. When two or three of them join together, a picture of sorts begins to emerge and comes to life. The darkness of the abyss takes on an ephemeral, living quality. But if looked at closely, the picture slowly begins to fade. Its meaning and importance are lost and the scraps of paper, separated once more, begin to swirl around and back into the pit of oblivion. Is it actually my own imagination which is attempting to join up those fragments and give them form? Do life's events conform to any fixed pattern, or does our desire for conformity cause our imagination to keep trying to give them a suitable form?

It seems that with my own hands I am opening several windows on to life.

Shadows and voices, colours—black and white and red—advancing and receding, begin to throng the imagination. Voices heard by the light of day fade away and lose their identity, there and then. But in the twilight and in the darkness of night, voices keep floating in the air and re-echoing from the walls, and even today it seems as if their reverberations are carried to me on the wind.

It is dusk. On one side of the courtyard, the tandoor is red hot and a lamp is burning in a niche outside the kitchen. Inside the kitchen, a cooking fire burns with a reddish glow. A member of the household comes out of the kitchen and, picking up the lamp from its niche, begins to cross the courtyard. Light and dark, suddenly interpenetrating, are shot through with life. Immensely long shadows are thrown on the walls. The circle of light around this person's legs keeps moving farther away.

The moment dusk falls, countless spectres and hobgoblins descend on the roof. And in every corner they peep at me from behind the doors.

'Alms! Give me alms!' The voice comes from a long, deserted lane at the back of the house. Now one hears the sound of a door opening. The door is opened. Footsteps are heard, but they stop. For a brief moment there is silence. Then there is a sound of the door closing and footsteps gradually receding. Soon afterwards, the same voice can be heard from far off down the lane: 'Alms! Give me alms!' Then silence reigns again. Who is this man who comes every night to ask for alms? Perhaps it is that same red-bearded man who goes about in the daytime with a long bag slung from his shoulder.

'*Pahar dandei!*' Another voice rends the darkness of the alley and, in its impenetrable gloom, a broad red formless mass begins to float. From the other end of the alley, this wind-borne shape keeps advancing. Is this a flame? Now, very soon, it will come closer, and then a voice will be heard, 'Pahar dandei!' And then I tremble from head to foot. Is this really a flame which is coming nearer by the second? No, no, it is a red rag tied to the end of a long stick carried by a mendicant, whose shaven head is smeared with oil. Again he calls out, 'Pahar dandei!'

And I, fearful and trembling, run to my mother, who is seated on a bedstead, and I cling to her legs. He appears to have held his stick up higher and the red shape, waving in the breeze, keeps coming closer and closer . . .

My eyes are closing. Before my half-closed eyes, a blackish mass of shapes is forming under the roof and is spreading out, growing in size. The shapes go on unfurling, but an 'Oh!' or an 'Ah!' from me causes them to shrivel away slowly, and the web of black, disordered lines condenses into a blackish blur. Now, in this form, it begins to float beneath the roof inside the room. Sometimes it goes up towards the roof and gets smaller. Then it comes down to me from the roof and assumes a persistently hideous form. If I utter another 'Oh!' it seems as if the light has been blotted out and the black blur is spreading again before my eyes as is the web of black disordered lines . . . My mother passes her hand over my head. She says, 'His forehead is burning.' I turn my head and again, light and dark masses alternately growing and shrinking, swirl in turn before my eyes . . .

I raise my hand and put it on my mother's lap. Passing her hand over my head, my mother says, 'Come, I'll sing you Moti Ram's all-seasons' song.' And patting my forehead, she begins to sing very softly, '*Oh my friend, try to understand that this world is illusory. Even your own kith and kin, with whom you have the strongest bonds of friendship, will one day go away from here.'*

I am quite familiar with this song. As Mother sings, her words bring different pictures to life before my eyes. As she sings the next lines, there rises before me the wall at the back of the house. A crow comes, sits on it and, a moment later, flies away and then starts hovering all around above the house. Mother sings: *'Take no pride in worldly things. They are just like the crow who comes and sits for a short time on the wall of your house and then flies away.'*

The crow has flown away but, now, Moti Ram with his small black moustache and his Peshawari turban appears, squatting on the ground. Mother goes on singing:

'Moti Ram says, *"Oh my friend, please remember that one day you will be set upon by the God of Death."'*

Mother's voice is uniformly sweet and her hand never stops patting my forehead. Now, when she sings, a black goat comes and stands before me, its head held high. Then, it seems as if somewhere at the back of the house, a pot has got broken—a large, earthenware dish.

Mother goes on to sing the stanza of the month of Baisakh: *'Forgetting the name of God'* (thus goes the couplet dedicated to the month of Baisakh, the second month of the Hindu year), *'you deck yourself out in finery, eat rich food and strut about; but, you are only like a goat being fattened up for the God of Death. This life is like a vessel which, in the end, must break to pieces . . .'*

After each stanza, Moti Ram, with his thin black moustache and Peshawari turban, quietly comes and sits before us.

'Moti Ram says, *"Oh my friend, you must realize that one day you will mingle with the dust."*'

From the lane, another voice can be heard, and my attention is distracted from my mother's sweet song. The voice is coming from the roof of the neighbouring house where Manohar lives. There too someone is singing but the words are different. And I feel as though I can see drops of water glistening and hear tiny bells ringing. Manohar's little sister's white kurta begins to shine and flutter in the moonlight and her hair starts to gleam.

> *We come flower-bedecked,*
> *In the cool weather!*
> *In the cool weather!*

Boys and girls are playing on the terrace of Manohar's house. It is half in darkness, half in moonlight. His three little sisters come forward in a row, from the darker half into the moonlight, with their arms around each other's waists, singing. The boys' row is standing facing them. Manohar and my brother Baldev are in it. And Suraj too is there. As the girls' row moves forward, singing, the boys' row gradually moves back.

> *We come flower-bedecked,*
> *In the cool weather!*

In the cool weather!

I know what will happen next. The boys' row will move forward, singing, and the girls' row will very slowly retreat.

> *Whom are you coming to get,*
> *In the cool weather?*
> *In the cool weather?*

Now the girls, singing, move forward:

> *We are coming to get Baldev,*
> *In the cool weather!*
> *In the cool weather!*
> *We are coming to get Baldev,*
> *In the cool weather!*

I already know that they will ask for Baldev. Every day they ask for Baldev, and only Baldev. I feel a stab of anguish and, putting my head on my mother's lap, I again turn over.

Baldev comes out of the boys' group and goes and joins the girls' group, and Manohar's little sister puts her arm around his waist. I again feel grief-stricken.

Tulsi is standing there, in a corner of the terrace. Manohar's sister doesn't allow him to play with them. 'You're a servant,' she says, 'your voice is coarse, like a buffalo's.' And all the girls start laughing. Manohar's sister doesn't let me play with her either. She says I'm too small.

So I, too—when I'm not ill—keep standing up against the parapet along with Tulsi.

I again toss and turn in my mother's lap. Mother goes on patting my forehead, and singing her *Barah Masa* song, the song of the twelve months. My attention has come back to Moti Ram's verses. Suddenly I hear the sound of my father's footsteps on the stairs. I utter a groan so that Mother will listen. Perhaps Father has come to look for his walking stick. Every evening he looks for it. He is sure to vent his anger on Mother. He must certainly have heard her singing but she continues to sing.

Father can be heard shouting, 'How many times have I told you not to sing songs of renunciation in front of the children? You just don't listen.'

Mother says gently, 'What can I do? I know only such songs and I find them so touching!'

'If that is so, you should sit by yourself and sing them. Don't sing them to the children.'

'I was singing Moti Ram's *Barah Masa*. What's wrong with that?'

'These are songs of despair. You should sing cheerful songs of hope to the children. They should be listening to the Vedic hymns. But you insist on singing sad songs. Such songs sung in the evening have a bad effect on the children's minds.'

'Why should they? May the Almighty give them long lives . . .'

'Enough, enough. Where is my walking stick? Have you seen it anywhere?' And Father goes off into another room to look for it.

'This house is so ill-kept that you can never find anything.' Then Father's voice comes from the other room, 'And nobody even answers when one asks.'

Mother removes my head from her lap. The clock on the wall starts chiming. I start counting. It has chimed ten times. On the tenth chime, Mother suddenly starts laughing. 'This whole house is topsy-turvy. It's still early evening but the clock is chiming ten o'clock.'

When Mother laughs, my whole world changes. Everything seems to lighten up and become easy. Her whole body shakes and I hide my head in her lap. Then I am afraid of nothing.

From high up under the eaves, Father can be heard calling, 'Tulsi! Have you seen my stick anywhere?'

'I'd better go and see to the cooking,' says Mother, heaving her plump body off the bedstead.

Someone can be heard coming up the stairs. They are my brother's footsteps. Now he's coming home after playing the whole evening.

Out of breath, he steps onto the landing at the head of the staircase, and right from there he starts shouting, 'Mother, Mother! I'm going out.' And searching for her, he comes into our room.

'Mother, we are going to the Gurukul Samaj.' Tulsi comes in right behind my brother.

In the dim evening light, it seems I am seeing Tulsi
Ram properly for the first time. Mentally, I start to squirm
with envy. It seems to me that he is standing behind my
brother and laughing. His swarthy complexion, button-
eyes and deep red gums are shining in the darkness. I don't
like him one little bit. Wherever he comes across me in the
house, he picks me up and throws me down.

'There's going to be an archery display. It's starting at
seven o'clock. I too am going,' says my brother, still panting.

'Is this any time to be going out? You've been playing
all day. Haven't you had your fill yet?'

I feel consoled when Mother says that my brother can't
go.

'Father has given me permission,' says my brother,
holding on to the edge of the bedstead and jumping up
and down.

'If that's what your father says, then why are you asking
me?'

'Father said, go and ask your mother.'

My brother and Tulsi both stand there. My brother's
fair complexion is glowing. Tulsi's face shows up broad and
swarthy and when he laughs, his deep red gums glisten.

'The whole day you keep roaming around and Tulsi is
becoming a good-for-nothing along with you.' My hopes
are raised again. Mother won't let my brother go. And
Tulsi won't be able to go either.

'Mother, he shoots his arrow at a thread with his eyes
closed, and breaks it. He has come from Lahore. I must go.'

Father's footsteps are coming nearer.

'The lamp hasn't been lighted and put in the room yet. Where on earth is Tulsi?'

Tulsi doesn't budge from where he's standing. When he hears Father's voice, why doesn't he go and light the lamp?

Father says, 'He wants to go and see the archery display. Can he go?'

'Look, my dear, just think. Is this the time to send the children out?'

'He can be sent along with Tulsi. Let him go and see the show. Where's the harm?'

'But, my dear, it is evening now and there is still so much work to be done. Who's going to help me out? Are you sending this little one also? You should think of what is right and proper.'

But Father is still looking for his stick, he pays no special attention to Mother's words—words on which my whole life depends.

Catching the last phrase, Father says: 'Let him go. Such people only come once in a while. The Gurukul Samaj isn't all that far away. He'll soon be back.' Father looks in every corner for his walking stick. 'The people at the Gurukul Samaj may not do any work worth the name, but they certainly put on good shows . . .'

'I too am going!' I shout.

Father comes to me. 'You too are going, you little rascal?'

Then, calling to Mother, he says, 'Let him go. Tulsi can carry him on his shoulders.'

'Look, my dear, please be practical. Should I send a sick child out? His forehead is burning.'

Up to this point, Mother had been my friend, and Father had been my foe. Now the positions had become reversed.

'His fever is very slight.' He puts his hand on my forehead.

'You shouldn't even think of sending him. You yourself spoil the children.'

'I too am going, I must go,' I say, sobbing.

'Let him go, let him go. It will cheer up the children. All they learn out in the streets is smutty songs. But if they go to the Samaj they'll hear something good.'

'I'm going, I'm going, I'm going!' I exclaim, clenching my fists.

Father goes off again into another room to look for his stick. This time he finds it. I can hear him saying, 'There it is! Who hung it up on the door? In this house a thing can be lying right there in front of everybody and nobody will tell you.'

'You are sending him out to see the show and you yourself are going out for a walk. Now it's getting late. When will you be back and when will I ever be finished with my work in the kitchen?'

'I'll be right back. I'll just take a round of the park and I'll come home. You can go and get the dinner ready.'

Father comes over to me. Gently stroking my forehead, he calls me little rascal. He takes all the change out of his pockets and puts it under my pillow. 'Get well and then I'll take you myself!' And he goes out of the room. Tulsi and my brother have run out of the room. Hot burning tears well up and begin to trickle from the corners of my eyes. Mother has got up and is on her way to the kitchen . . .

I can hear laughter coming from the kitchen. It is my two elder sisters. Sisters? No, they are two white fairies who keep roaming around the house together, constantly running from room to room.

Through my tears, my gaze again becomes fixed on the roof. Now the face of the bearded raja doesn't appear between two beams. Nor can I see the horse which runs in front of him. A web of lines again floats before my eyes. Spreading out, it becomes enlarged. It goes on expanding. If I utter an 'Oh!' or an 'Ah!' it will start to dwindle. It will go on shrinking until finally it turns into a black blur and it will remain so, floating in the air.

∽

The sun is up. By the light of day, everything becomes natural, stable and familiar. But when night falls, frightening shadows flit past on every side. I come downstairs holding Mother's hand. Mother opens the door. He is standing there in front of us—the mendicant who had shouted in the night. I start trembling from head to foot, but no, it's not the same fakir. This man is wearing a long, loose, green garment, and he has a white beard. Nor does he carry a long stick with a flaming torch at the end.

'Put it in, son, put it in my bag!' The fakir opens wide a large bag and holds it out in front of me. I don't budge from where I'm standing. I just keep staring fixedly at his face.

'Go on, put it in, son. Don't be afraid,' says Mother. 'The holy man won't hurt you!'

I step forward, throw both the bowl and the wheat flour into the holy man's bag and then cling to Mother. But I'm not trembling. The old man laughs, and his long yellowish teeth show through his beard. Taking the bowl out of his bag, he comes towards me. 'May Allah grant you a long life! May your house prosper!'

'Take it, son. Take the bowl,' says Mother. Keeping my eyes on his yellow teeth, I take the bowl. I'm not the slightest bit afraid. He extends his hand and fondles my head. Even then I don't tremble.

'Sing something for us, Babaji,' Mother says to him. And the holy man takes a small, one-stringed instrument off his shoulder, holds it near his ear and, closing his eyes and tilting his head, he starts to sing:

'*Oh dear children of God, go into the towns and tell the people that this life is transient. Oh God! Inscrutable are your ways! You change flowing streams into a desert, and where there is a desert, you cause the streams to flow.*'

The baba has turned around and, walking very slowly, has gone off into the lane on the left. I've heard this song before on several occasions, and I know it by heart. My brother too knows it and so do my mother and my sisters. But today is the first time I have set eyes on this singing holy man. As we go upstairs, the song can be heard from the lane:

'*Don't say that this world is mine or yours. You are here in this world only for a short time and all that will be left of you is a handful of dust. Dear children of God, go into the towns and tell the people that this life is transient.*'

The whole day at home I keep moving from one room to another. This is the old *sufa*, the large living room. It's full of beds. The bed up against the wall is mine and my brother's. Before going to sleep, I quarrel with him and pinch him. I scratch the backs of his hands with my nails and in that way I get my revenge for his indifferent behaviour towards me during the day. But I don't get any response from him. He turns his back to me and goes to sleep.

This cupboard in the wall, with one of its doors always hanging open, is my sisters'. The chalk lines on its doors are their handiwork.

Behind the old sufa, there is a little closet we call the prayer room. This too has a cupboard in which books are kept, but they are not ordinary books. They are the holy writ, the Vedas, which always have newspaper covers on them.

Both my sisters are standing in front of the cupboard and asking each other, 'How many Vedas are there in all?' 'Four.' 'How many subordinate branches?' 'Ten.' Then Vidya, my elder sister, counts on her fingers and says, 'Rigveda has a daughter and that daughter has a son. The third Veda, Samveda, has a daughter and that daughter has a son. That way, it comes to eight, but you say there are ten?'

'There are ten. Panditji says there are ten.'

On one side of the sufa next to my sisters' cupboard, there is a door opening into another room, which is always closed. There is a very big cupboard in which are kept a pencil box and a device for relieving headaches. There is also a knife with a gold-plaited handle, which Father allows us to hold and look at, but which he takes back again before closing the room.

Right outside the sufa is the staircase landing, with a balustrade in front. If you stand near it on tiptoe, you can look down. But if you spit over it, Father will scold you. And now, down there in the courtyard, stands Father, asking for curds. 'Baldev's mother, let me have some curds so that I can go and have a bath.'

Mother comes out of the kitchen, leans over the balustrade and says, 'Look, will you please be reasonable? Here I am, serving the food, and you are going to have a bath!'

'Why must you always argue with me? If you have any curds, send it down to me. If there isn't any, just say so. I'll only take a minute to bathe and then I'll be there.'

ॐ

This is the painter's cupboard. (My brother finds fault with the way I pronounce 'painter's' and makes me repeat the word over and over again.) Even when I stand on tiptoe, I can't see inside it. Whenever Mother's keys go missing, Father calls from downstairs, 'Look in the painter's cupboard. That's where they'll be.' It's that very cupboard.

The painter's. But I can't see anything inside it except a discoloured green box. Are Mother's keys kept in this box? Who puts them there?

Downstairs is Father's office. There he sits the whole day long, bespectacled, tapping on his typewriter with one finger. If Tulsi goes near him he gets a scolding. There's a clock on the wall which chimes the half-hour, not like the one upstairs which only chimes the hour. Stretched above the fireplace is a long black cloth with I don't know how many peacocks on it, standing one behind the other—red, yellow, green peacocks. They look as if they were all running after each other. There is also a picture of Swamiji. In this one he has clothes on. In the picture upstairs, he is sitting in the nude and has a tiger and a snake behind him. There is also an animal that resembles the son of my father's younger brother's wife. My sister says, 'You see? Swamiji was never afraid of anything or anybody, not even a tiger or a cheetah.'

Right next to the office is another room, which is for shutting me up in. Whenever I utter the word 'sister fucker' in the lane or the street, Tulsi comes and tells Mother, and I get shut up in this room. When I'm inside it, I stand at the window and keep looking out into the lane. Then Mother comes and opens the door. She grips my head between her knees and puts a pinch of red chilli powder into my mouth. Then she goes back without a word. I stay squirming by the window. After being shut up for some time, I am let out, and the very moment I'm out, I start pummelling my brother.

Downstairs, behind the bathroom, is the garage where the cow is kept tethered. Tulsi sings here. He comes into the bathroom to prepare the cow's feed and, with bits of straw sticking to his huge hands, he starts to sing in a loud voice.

'That's enough now,' says Mother to him, laughing. 'I have no peace at all with you on one side of me and the washerman's ass on the other.'

I can't sing like Tulsi, but I can do something else. I go to the tandoor, pick up an empty can and place it upside down, right in the centre of the courtyard. Then, banging on it with a stick, I start shouting, 'Arise, Muslims, and keep your fast!'

The sound of the tin box being banged can be heard far and wide. Encouraged by this thought, I beat the can even harder, and shout even more loudly, 'Arise, Muslims, and keep your fa-a-ast!' From behind the house, a woman's voice calls, 'Hey, Lakshmi, your son would have us keep our *roza*, the fast of Ramadan, all the year round!' And she laughs. Sometimes, Mother calls back to her from where she's sitting in the kitchen, and at other times she gets up, comes out into the courtyard, stands on top of the tandoor and peeps into the neighbour's house. Mother and the neighbour have a long conversation while I keep drumming on my tin box.

If you stand out on the balcony, you can see a canal at one end of the street where tonga drivers wash down their horses and where Manohar, Inder and Girdhari catch wasps. If you look along the street in the other direction, you won't find anything eye-catching. The end of the street isn't visible. My world begins at the canal and goes only as far as the shop of Attar Singh, the sweetmeat seller, where some people have spread out a rug at the edge of the street and are playing a game of *chaupat* using shells for dice. I have no idea of what lies beyond.

At the front of the house, when the shadow of the building gradually steals across to the other side of the street, the afternoon has begun. Mother spreads my bed out on the balcony. Putting her hand on my forehead, she says, 'Get well quickly and then you can play all you want.'

The water-carrier has filled his first leather water-bag from the canal. Stooping under the weight of the bag slung across his back, he comes along, sprinkling the road with water in short bursts, controlling the mouth of the bag with one hand and directing the flow of water with the other. One half of the road seems to have a shadow spreading across it, and from it comes the fragrance of water-drenched soil. If I hadn't been ill, I'd have been walking along right behind the water-carrier just to smell it. Having got as far as Maulvi Ishaq's house with the now-shrunken bag hanging from his shoulder, the water-carrier straightens up. He turns around and takes his bag back to the canal to fill it up again.

Right in front of our house, Fez Ali has unhitched the horse from his tonga, and the bamboo shafts are now pointing skywards, just as, whenever it is prayer time, Maulvi Ishaq's arms are raised heavenwards. The horse is still in harness and Fez Ali's son, holding its bridle, brings it right into the centre of the road.

Under the harness, the horse's back, blackened with sweat, keeps twitching. To brush away the flies sitting on its back, the horse flicks its tail over and over again. Even so, they keep rising in swarms. The horse of its own accord starts moving into the middle of the road. Fez Ali's son has gone back into the house. Very slowly, the horse will reach Attar Singh's sweetmeat shop, then, it will turn round and come back to Fez Ali's cot, on the edge of the street in front of his house. Then, once again, it will turn and go back up to Attar Singh's shop. Fez Ali has taken off his khaki-coloured turban and, sitting on his cot, he puffs away at a hookah with quiet satisfaction.

Girdhari sits at the end of the lane, on top of a stone fixed in the ground, legs dangling. Holding a *gulli—a* small wooden piece, pointed at each end—in one hand and swinging a *danda*—a short stick—in the other, he starts yelling, 'Come and play gulli-danda!' This invitation to play is for me, my brother and the other neighbourhood boys. He keeps rapping the stick on the stone and shouting, 'Come and play gulli-danda!' I keep turning over in my bed.

At the manger, there are children sitting around on the wet ground catching wasps. Inder can catch wasps with his bare hands. Holding the wasp in one hand, he removes its sting with two fingers of the other hand, then, after attaching a thread to its legs, he sends it flying. The wasp flies up a little, then falls to the ground. Tethered, it can't reach the sky as a *patang*—kite—can.

From the lane where Girdhari is sitting, calling everyone to come and play gulli-danda, a burqa-clad woman comes into the street. The moment she leaves the lane, she drops her veil over her face and walks along the street. Once across the street, she will slip into the lane next to our house and, as she does so, she will lift her veil. This is what all the burqa-clad women do. Walking on the street, they drop their veils. Walking along the lane, they lift them up.

Next to our house, five horses belonging to the Chhachhi tonga drivers are tethered by the roadside. Here and there in the neighbourhood, tongas, unhitched from their horses, their bamboo poles pointing upwards, are standing. As always, cots have been placed in front of the *kothari* of an old, lame man called Baba Nooroo. All the elderly tonga drivers of the neighbourhood—Fateh Khan, Jilani, Karam Khan, Mohammad Din—sit there and chat. Fateh Din, sitting beside the alley tap, is changing the water of the hookah. First, really filthy water comes out, then yellow-coloured, then clean water. He blows so forcefully through the hookah pipe that his cheeks puff out and the veins in his forehead swell. My cheeks could never puff out as much as his. I cover my mouth with the back of my hand and blow, but neither do my cheeks puff out nor do the veins on my forehead swell. Karam Khan's son, who is sitting at the edge of the gutter, is mixing a jaggery sherbet in an earthen vessel, next to the tonga drivers' cots. The Chhachhis will drink the sherbet from tiny, shallow earthenware bowls, and, turn by turn, will puff at the one hookah that does the rounds. There they will stay in quiet conversation until nightfall.

Nawab Khan, Subedar Jalal Khan's son, has come out of the lane and is sauntering along the middle of the street. He goes for a stroll at this time every day. Mother says he ambles along. The crest of his white turban flaps about in the wind. The salwar he wears is also white and rustles as he walks. Below it, are black, shiny shoes. Like Fez Ali's horse, he too strolls from the manger to Attar Singh's shop and back. But he walks slowly, holding himself very erect, and keeps twisting the ends of his jet-black moustache. Now, his tonga driver will harness the horse to the tonga and bring it in front of our house. In the whole neighbourhood, no one has quite such a well-polished tonga as this. It is black with white stripes, and the horse has tall plumes on its head and a gleaming black harness on its back. The roof of the tonga is removable. The whip, standing in its holder, tapers towards the end, so that its top half bends over and hangs down. My brother says it's not a whip, it's a hunter.

The subedar's son, holding the reins, has leapt into the front seat of the tonga. Both the end of the whip and the crest of his turban are flying high in the wind. The tonga driver is sitting in the rear seat. The horse, arching its neck, moves forward with a clattering of hooves. The people sitting at old, lame Baba Nooroo's kothari turn their heads and look in that direction. Everyone in the neighbourhood is afraid of Nawab Khan. Without reason or warning, he catches hold of somebody or the other and starts beating them up.

'Come and play gulli-danda!' Girdhari is still shouting.

From the left, near the manger, a herd of cows comes running from around the corner. Mahmooda, wielding a staff, comes running along, right behind the herd. His flailing staff lands now on one cow, now on another. His kurta buttons are always open, so that his pale, white body can be seen from afar.

Both my sisters are standing at one end of the *chhajja*, the balcony facing the road. When did they come? Seeing them, I get confused. How long have they been standing there? They don't talk to me. They just keep whispering to each other. But I know what they're talking about. Opposite our house, two houses away, is Surasti's house. Surasti is my sisters' friend. When I'm not ill, I go at my sisters' bidding to call Surasti. In the meantime, I catch the sound of heavy footsteps behind me. Father has come up on to the chhajja to take my temperature. My heart begins to thump. As he puts the thermometer into my mouth, his gaze falls on my sisters.

'Vidya! Vimla!' he says sharply. The thermometer quivers in my mouth. 'What are you doing standing here? Haven't I told you several times not to come on to the chhajja?'

Both my sisters duck their heads and run away from there. They are not allowed to come on to the chhajja. Nor can they look out of the windows of the old or the new sufas. And they can't stand on the roof of the house. And if they laugh out loud, Father scolds them. 'Vidya! Vimla! Just let me catch you raising your voices! Sit down nicely and be quiet.'

And Vidya and Vimla immediately fall silent. But I know for a fact they can never stifle their laughter. My little sister Vimla doesn't laugh much, but my big sister Vidya keeps laughing all the time. Whenever Tulsi appears, they both start giggling loudly.

Round the clock, Tulsi and we children are inseparable. In the afternoon, when Panditji comes to give us our tuition, he keeps sitting the whole time in the corridor. In the evening when my brother plays on the roof with a bow and arrow, Tulsi too plays with us. When we compete at pegging by the roadside outside the house, he joins in. My brother has driven a nail into the end of a long stick, with the point of the nail on the outside, to make a javelin. Javelin in hand, Tulsi comes running from the manger and, when he comes close to the house, he shouts out, 'Ya Ali!' Then he swings the stick about, his *chutia*, topknot, dancing all the while. Then, pointing the nail end forward, he takes aim. A dried cow dung cake has been set up as a target outside the house with the help of a brick. If the aim is correct, the javelin goes right through it. Sometimes the nail gets stuck in the cake. Then the javelin thrower, like a triumphant warrior, comes back to his place, swinging it above his head.

When my brother mixes sawdust with gum to make a printing press, Tulsi and I grind up pieces of coal to make ink for it. Whenever Tulsi is with us, no one in the entire neighbourhood has the courage to pick a quarrel with us. He strikes his head against the fellow's chest, and sinks his teeth into the assailant's arm. 'He's a brute,' my mother always says. 'He's not a human being, he's an animal.' My sisters always laugh at everything he says.

Sitting in the corridor outside the kitchen, Tulsi says in his raucous voice, 'In the village, we wash our heads with dal.' My sisters look at each other and laugh. Then Vidya quietly gets up and goes into the kitchen. Picking up the cooking pot of left-over dal, she empties it right over Tulsi's head. 'Wash your head, Tulsi!' And the dal begins to trickle down to his ears. 'What are you doing?' he says, jumping up. And both my sisters roll about on the floor with laughter.

Other scenes connected with Tulsi begin to come before my eyes. He is coming running from the opposite lane. Blood is streaming down from his forehead onto his face and neck, and his kurta has drops of blood on it. Before he can reach the end of the lane, a stone hits him in the back. He manages to take only a few more steps when, one after another, two stones come flying, one of which hits him again in his back. Tulsi's hand goes straight to his back and feels his wound. He picks up a stone from the ground, turns around and throws it into the lane, and then, he runs back into the lane and disappears from view.

'This has started happening every day,' Mother, standing on the chhajja, mutters. 'He is a brute; gets involved in scuffles every day. But then, your father . . .'

Father is standing in the kitchen, wiping his face with a towel. 'What's the matter?' he asks.

'Look, my dear, just give this some thought. Houses have been built up all around here. Where is Tulsi supposed to go to ease himself?'

'What happened?'

'Look, my dear, Tulsi goes back there to the graveyard to ease himself. If he goes in the dark, nobody sees him. But at the first ray of light, they pelt him with stones to drive him away. Let him go where every member of the family goes, and then this daily problem will be avoided.'

'But can't he go earlier?' Father mutters. 'He eats too much. Eight rotis at each meal. These people are dirty.' Father can't stand the idea of Tulsi going 'upstairs' to ease himself.

To the end, he could not stand the idea of Tulsi using the same latrine as everyone else.

While we three are playing on the roof, we stop and look towards the mountains. Some distance away, to the left of our house, there is a hill which sometimes looks blue and at other times looks bright red. Today, with the rain, it can be seen very clearly and appears to have come closer. Every single thing has been washed clean. Even trees and large rocks stand out individually. Crows in their hundreds are flying from there towards the town. It's the same story every day. Early in the morning, they come flying over and, as soon as night falls, they fly back to the hill.

'What's beyond this hill?' asks my brother.

I look towards him. 'There's nothing at all beyond it.' I couldn't even imagine that there might be anything beyond it.

'There's London on the other side of the hill,' he says. Tulsi and I search my brother's face.

Then Tulsi shakes his head. 'No, no, behind this hill there is Rumli,' he says.

'What's Rumli?'

'Rumli is my village.' And, suddenly, Tulsi puts his head between his knees and starts sobbing convulsively.

I have not seen Rumli. But I have seen Tulsi's uncle—his father's younger brother—who sometimes comes from there. He is tall and very thin and has a red moustache. I have also seen Tulsi's younger brother. He comes occasionally from the village. My sisters make fun of him too by hiding something or the other belonging to him. Nobody else comes from Rumli. Only these two come and go.

The three of us go upstairs. Next to the painter's cupboard, my sisters are standing shoulder to shoulder, crying without stopping. Throughout the house there is silence—no churning of buttermilk, no pounding of pestle and mortar to prepare the chutney.

'What has happened?' asks my brother of my younger sister. She starts sobbing even louder. But the older sister says very softly, 'A man hit our father and broke his finger.'

I don't understand but my heart begins to throb violently. The three of us go without a sound to the old sufa. On the cot placed in front of the windows, our father is sitting with his legs dangling. Mother is sitting beside him on the cot and fanning him.

I go straight to Father and stand in front of him. He looks up in my direction and gives a slight smile. He has a big bandage on one finger. I keep looking at it.

Father says gently, 'I got hurt.'

I watch his face in silence. I can't think of our father being injured.

He looks again in my direction and says smiling, 'A man sprained my finger. He started quarrelling with me and twisted it.'

That somebody could twist my father's finger was difficult for me to imagine. He was the tallest person in the house and talked so commandingly. Why didn't he reprimand the man? If he had done so, the man would definitely have let go of Father's finger.

'Where does this vegetable seller park his cart?' Mother asks.

'Opposite the Gurukul Samaj.'

'How would it have mattered if you got one cucumber less? For your own sake, if he didn't agree, you should have asked him to weigh everything again,' Mother mutters.

Father just keeps sitting there with his head bowed as before. He has turned quite pale. Trembling, I keep watching his face in fear. But I am inwardly seething against that unknown man. I feel like going and beating him up. I want to pull his hair and hear him shriek. I want to throw his turban down on the ground.

'Shall I bring some gruel?' Mother asks, bending forward. 'Have a little gruel.'

Father silently shakes his head.

'Where is Tulsi?' Mother asks and she suddenly becomes anxious. 'Where is Tulsi? Have you sent him anywhere, my dear?'

Tulsi had come upstairs with us. But now he isn't in the room.

'No, I haven't sent him anywhere,' says Father, shaking his head.

'Vidya,' Mother calls out. 'Go and see where Tulsi is. He must be sitting downstairs somewhere. Don't let him go out.'

Mother gets up in a flurry. My elder sister runs off downstairs. My younger sister comes and stands in the corridor. Even now she is weeping softly.

'He must be on the chhajja,' says my brother, and goes to look for him there.

Tulsi is nowhere in the house. Mother, greatly concerned, keeps shaking her head. 'My heart is beating hard,' she says. 'He is going to bring trouble down upon us. Look, Vidya, how my heart is pounding.' And Mother takes Vidya's hand and puts it on her heart.

'You feel it?'

'Yes, Mother.'

When Vidya takes her hand away, I put my hand on Mother's heart, but I don't feel it thumping.

'Go and play. There's nothing wrong with me,' says Father to me, at the same time, affectionately dismissing my brother and sisters.

Throughout the entire house there is an atmosphere of gloom. Father stays in the room. I come out and sit down to do Panditji's work, but, from behind the door, I keep glancing in Father's direction. He is lying down, either gazing at the ceiling or lifting his bandaged hand and examining it.

Mother has come out of the room and sits down to churn the curds. Both my sisters sit distractedly outside the kitchen. It is starting to get hot. So I leave the shelter of the door and go and sit down in front of the new sufa. Father, it seems, has gone to sleep.

After some time, my brother comes running down from the chhajja to announce: 'Tulsi's back, he's coming!'

I throw down my slate and run to the chhajja. Both my sisters also rush upstairs, but Mother stops them.

'Vidya, Vimla, you're not to go. Sit where you are.'

We can't see Tulsi from the chhajja. We both come back in and rush towards the staircase. Tulsi is climbing the stairs very slowly, holding on to the wall. He appears to be ill. In one hand, Tulsi is holding two cucumbers.

Without saying a word, Tulsi comes upstairs and sits down in the kitchen doorway, holding his head. His eyes are swollen and there is a lump on his forehead. Seeing this, Mother bites her lip, and, shaking her head, she says, 'This is exactly what I was afraid of.' Then placing both the earthenware vessels for churning buttermilk on her knees, she says, 'Who told you to go there? Why did you set foot out of the house?'

Tulsi still sits in the doorway, silently clutching his head with both his hands. Seeing him sitting like that, both my sisters burst out laughing.

'Poor thing,' murmurs my younger sister, and puts her hand over her mouth to stifle her laughter. 'My goodness, Vidya, be quiet, Father will hear you.' For a moment both fall silent, but suddenly their giggles burst forth again and, falling against each other, they become quite helpless with laughter.

Dropping his hands from his swollen eyes, Tulsi looks at my sisters and says abruptly, 'Blood is flowing from his teeth too. There were three of them, but I was alone. I butted him in the chest and bit so deep into his arm that he's not likely to forget me. I also twisted his fingers.'

Both my sisters fall silent. In my heart of hearts, I am glad that he has paid back the person who had twisted my father's finger.

'I've also brought two of his cucumbers,' he says, addressing them. 'I first took four cucumbers, then he came running after me, so I threw two into the gutter.' A slight grin appears on Tulsi's face. 'The next time he twists Father's finger, I'll lop off his ear.'

'That's enough. Be quiet. You're a brute,' says Mother. 'Get up, Vidya, take the gruel off the fire, pour it into a bowl and give it to Tulsi.'

'But Mother, that's for Father.'

'It doesn't matter. Pour half of it into a bowl and give it to him.'

Tulsi has risen high in my esteem. He seems very brave. He has not only thrashed Father's enemy, but has also brought away his cucumbers.

Mother picks up both the cucumbers and goes towards the sufa to show them to Father, but she comes back after merely peeping through the door. The atmosphere in the house has lightened somewhat.

Some time later, Tulsi explains to us two brothers the tricks of wrestling: 'First of all, butt him right in the chest, then cling to him. Your enemy won't be able to do anything. Don't ever catch him by the hair. If you catch him by the hair, he'll catch you by your topknot. Then what will you do? First of all, butt him, butt him right in the chest, and then bite his arm. Your enemy will be helpless.'

Wagging his head, my brother said, 'That's how the Rajputs used to fight, but they also had swords and shields.' He has a book titled, *The Twilight of the Rajputs*. He has learnt a great deal from it. 'But they never attacked from the rear, and if an enemy fell down, they did not strike him either.'

'Did they butt enemies with their heads?' asks Tulsi.

'I don't know.' After looking at Tulsi for a long time, my brother said, 'It's not written in the book.'

'They must surely have butted opponents with their heads,' insists Tulsi. 'Did they have hair on their heads?'

'I don't know.' My brother, again looking at Tulsi, says, 'It's not written in the book.'

The sound of the downstairs door clicking can be heard.

'Go. Your tutor, Panditji, has come,' says Vidya, looking at my brother. 'Tulsi, go and open the door for him.'

Mother cuts in with, 'Let Tulsi be, daughter. Get up, Baldev, go downstairs and study in the office.'

I open my mouth to say that my stomach is hurting, but I know that Mother will not believe this and both my sisters will start laughing, so I quietly get up and follow my brother.

We both sit down on the *durrie*. Panditji sits down in the chair in front of us with one leg up on the seat. My eyes are fixed on his thin, quivering lips through which now and again his tiny, worn-down teeth gleam. He constantly thrusts his lips forward when he is speaking. When he is teaching, he removes his turban and this suddenly makes him look very small.

'I get in all eleven rupees as salary.' Every second or third day, Panditji repeats this.

Then he asks my brother, 'Have you memorized the Sanskrit couplet?'

'Yes,' comes Baldev's prompt reply.

'What does it say?'

'Brother should not hate brother, sister should not hate sister . . .'

'Well done! Do you two brothers eat off the same plate?'

'Yes, sir,' says my brother.

'Do you sleep on one bed?'

'Yes, sir.'

'Do you play together?'

'Yes, sir.'

'And how do you walk? Beside each other, or one behind the other?'

My brother doesn't understand the question. Nor do I. Panditji explains: 'You should walk ahead, while your brother should walk behind. Ram and Laxman used to walk like that.'

'He pinches me,' complains my brother.

Panditji fixes his weasel gaze on me.

'You pinch your elder brother?'

I keep quiet.

'Your little brother is very naughty, that's why he's skinny. Good boys are healthy.' Having said this, Panditji points to a chart hanging on the wall and tells my brother to read it.

Every third or fourth day, Panditji has my brother read from this chart. Both of us know it by heart.

'Simplicity is life, ostentation is death.'

'What does that mean?'

'It means you shouldn't have any hair on your head.' My brother quickly adds, 'And you shouldn't shave off your moustache. Nowadays, people shave off their moustaches and grow their hair very long. That is death.' My brother has memorized the answers given to him by Panditji.

'Read on.'

'Rectitude is life. Misconduct is death.'

'What does that mean?'

In the meantime, Tulsi comes quietly, as he does every day, and sits down in the doorway. The three of us gaze at Panditji: 'This means that you should look down at women's feet. You should not look at their faces.'

'What is misconduct?'

'Misconduct means touching the place from where your urine comes out. Swearing too is misconduct,' says my brother. 'But, Panditji, my little brother puts his hand on that place.'

Panditji's narrow eyes open wide and he goes on looking into my face. In a very low voice, he asks me: 'Do you really put your hand on the place from where your urine comes out?'

'Yes, sir,' I say, nodding my head. 'I can even make it large.'

Panditji's leg comes down off the chair and my face receives a resounding smack which makes my head spin.

'You sinner! You villain! This boy is very bad.'

Even then I understand nothing. It is as if everything round me has become squinty and wobbly.

'This is a very bad thing to do. You will get worms in your penis. And in your hands too. Do you understand?'

I still can't understand anything. I feel afraid and keep watching Panditji's small slit eyes. The pain from the blow on my cheek is lessening somewhat. Looking into Panditji's stony eyes, I become frightened, just as I do when Father rebukes me.

'Open your book,' says Panditji to my brother. My brother takes his book out of his schoolbag.

'Read!'

My brother starts reading.

Tulsi, still with his chin on his knees, continues to listen as he mumbles the words.

'Now give the meaning,' says Panditji. Then addressing Tulsi, he says, 'You haven't brought the buttermilk yet, Tulsi?'

While Panditji drinks it, the lesson stops for a short while, which is a great consolation. My brother starts to explain the Sanskrit couplet. But even then I keep watching Panditji's face. Wouldn't it be just great, I thought to myself, if Mother taught him a lesson by not sending down any buttermilk.

'Even when she saw . . . her son . . . falling into the fire, the virtuous wife did not awaken her husband . . .'

Tulsi has brought the glass of buttermilk.

'You haven't put any butter in it today, Tulsi Ram.' Panditji smiles and speaks softly, just as he does when he is asking Father for money.

'Mother forgot to put it in. I'll bring it.' And he retraces his steps.

Panditji sips the buttermilk. My gaze remains fixed on the rise and fall of his Adam's apple, and I go on watching him like this without blinking. Panditji is very fortunate. He has such a big Adam's apple. Something which I don't have. But my brother doesn't have one either, and knowing that is a consolation. The Adam's apple goes on bobbing up and down.

From the upstairs balustrade comes the sound of Mother grumbling: 'Does drinking plain lassi give him a pain in the stomach? He wants butter every day. Ugh! Go . . . take it from the bowl.'

Panditji is sipping buttermilk with his eyes closed. Then, as he waits for the butter, he opens his eyes and looks at us.

'There are thirty-two compartments in the stomach,' he says. 'Each day's food goes into a separate compartment. Today's food will go into today's compartment.' Having said this, Panditji closes his tiny eyes and wags his head. 'It's just like the buckets on a chain in a well which, turn by turn, get filled up and emptied!' Panditji again closes his eyes and wags his head.

Tulsi has brought the butter in a small bowl. Panditji puts it into the glass of buttermilk and then, with each sip, he uses his dark brown fingers to put some into his mouth. I am imagining that the compartment into which the buttermilk and butter are falling must be right underneath his Adam's apple.

But my gaze strays from Panditji's Adam's apple to his very wide nostrils behind which the bone of his nose disappears. Suddenly, I pipe up, 'Panditji, did a railway train run through your nose?'

The glass of buttermilk stops in mid-air. Panditji's leg again comes down off the chair. Speechless, Panditji looks me in the face. 'What did you say?' he asks, his tiny eyes widening till they look enormous.

'A railway train ran through your nose, my sister says—right through your nose.'

'That will do, you silly boy!' Having said this, he leans back in the chair.

'You silly boy!' I repeat.

Panditji bends towards me, reaches out, takes hold of my left ear and begins to squeeze it gently. At first I keep on laughing, then suddenly I squeal. Initially, Panditji catches hold of my ear, tickles it, then gently rubs it and massages it, then he suddenly tweaks it, at which point I howl.

'You don't say such things to your teacher, do you understand? That too is misconduct.'

But I get up, feeling very upset, and go weeping to Tulsi who, I think, will get up and, as is usual with him, attack Panditji by butting him in the chest. But he sits right where he is.

'You don't talk like that to your teacher,' he says in a deep, gruff voice. 'Sit down beside me.' And, putting his hand on my shoulder, he makes me sit next to him.

When the lesson is over, I go straight upstairs to Mother. She is sitting outside the kitchen making balls of dough to put into the tandoor.

'I won't study with this Pandit!' I shout. 'He beats me!'

Mother can see it from the redness of my ear.

'My goodness! How dare he strike a small child—the butcher!' And, in a rage, she gets up from beside the plate in which she is kneading dough and rushes to the balustrade. In the meantime, Tulsi and my brother have come upstairs.

'Has your tutor left?'

'Yes, he has.'

'Why did he hit him? Why didn't you come and tell me? Does he come here to thrash my children?'

'No, Mother, it's his fault,' says my brother. 'He puts his hand where his urine comes out.'

Mother stares at me. Her eyes open very wide, like Panditji's. And the tip of her tongue shows through her clenched teeth. Mother keeps looking at me.

'Do you do such dirty things?' she asks me, her whole expression changing. 'Come here and I'll set you right!' And, advancing on me, she catches me by the hand.

'Just bring the pepper pot, Tulsi.'

And sitting down on the stool, she wedges my face between her knees as she always does.

'Now, speak up. Will you ever do such dirty things again?'

This change in Mother has come about so quickly that I go on looking at her even more stupidly than before.

Tulsi has brought the pepper pot.

'Speak up. Will you ever do dirty things like that again?'

On such occasions, if you shake your head and say, 'No!' loudly enough, Mother will sometimes let you off. But I am still staring into her face.

'All right, be off with you. You've had enough beating for one day.' And she releases my head from the vice-like grip of her knees.

'Mother,' says my brother, 'Panditji said that boys who put their hands where their urine comes out from get infested with worms.'

'What kind of a person is this Panditji of yours? He keeps on saying such nasty things.'

After Panditji has left, I sit downstairs in a corner of the courtyard. I distractedly think that the man who sits at the edge of the gutter near the Gurukul Samaj, both his legs swollen and smeared with oil, must definitely have kept touching where his urine comes from—that was why his legs are swollen, and you can see things like worms crawling about on them. And that lame fakir, too, with the crooked gait, who comes to our neighbourhood . . .

Tulsi comes downstairs to me.

'I didn't tell about the other thing, now, did I?' says Tulsi, by way of consolation. I look at him. 'You know, about the railway train. We won't tell Mother about that.'

Feeling distraught, I stand up and, to get away from him, go up to the chhajja. For many days after that, I am afraid that those two may mention my second sin to Mother.

In our house, everybody can recite the mantras of the prayers by heart. In the daytime both my sisters vie with each other over who can recite all the mantras the fastest. Mother sits on the chhajja to say her prayers with her head and face covered with her dupatta. Father often prays in his own room but, in the evening, before dinner, he sometimes says his prayers in the kitchen itself. Then, he is the first to finish his prayers, even before my sisters. When he closes his eyes, all of us children keep quiet, but Mother, who sits beside the cooking fire, remains involved with the utensils. Whenever Father dines late, he says his prayers right there in the kitchen. Seeing him close his eyes, Mother takes a platter and two small bowls from the fireplace and puts a chapatti on the *tava*. The moment the chapatti comes off the tava, and the dal and vegetables have been put into the bowl, Father bows his head and says, 'Om, Shanti, Shanti' and he opens his eyes. Then, pulling the plate towards him, he says:

'We thank you! We thank you, Oh Lord!'

We have the benefit of hearing these words fall from Father's lips several times during the day—in the early morning when it is time to get up, at mealtimes and at bedtime.

Father has no fixed time for saying prayers. If he can't say his prayers in the morning, he says them in the afternoon. He says the early morning prayers in his room. On hot summer days, he sits on a prayer mat spread on the floor and prays with his back against the wall. But on cold winter days, he prays sitting on the bed. During the morning prayers Father often dozes off and, when his chin remains lowered down to his neck for a long time, we understand that he has finished the prayers and is bowing his head in the final obeisance. Shortly afterwards, he raises his head with a start and his eyes open for an instant, but then he becomes immobile again in the posture of prayer.

Sometimes, holy men come to our house, especially at the time of the Arya Samaj anniversary. Then, we two brothers, wearing khaki shirts and shorts, look after the innumerable pairs of shoes laid out in rows, and give the members of the audience water to drink and fan them with the huge fans we carry. On the day of the *nagar kirtan*, the procession singing religious songs through the streets, we always perch ourselves on some bullock cart or the other, on which a chair and table have been placed for some good singer. During that period, holy men and preachers come to our house every day and have their meals with us. After the meal, Mother sits at their feet and says, 'Oh holy master, I can't keep my mind on my prayers. Tell me of some remedy. When I close my eyes, my mind darts here and there. How can I cure myself of this?'

The holy men say, shaking their heads, 'Devi! Do *pranayama*, the alternate inhalation and exhalation through the left and right nostrils. From pranayama, will come resolution.'

From that day, Mother goes and sits on the chhajja with her head and face wrapped in her dupatta. With the forefinger of her right hand, she closes her left nostril and breathes in. Then with the forefinger of her left hand, she closes her right nostril and breathes out. Standing a little way off, we four children stand with bulging eyes, watching to see if she has become resolute or not. But after a few days, Mother stops sitting on the chhajja and, the next time a *sadhu* comes to our house, she says, 'Holy master, I perform pranayama and I also carry out every kind of religious observance, but, even so, I can't concentrate on my prayers.'

The holy man shakes his head and says, 'Devi, recite mantras with a rosary. Recite the *gayatri mantra* one hundred and eight times with the rosary in your hand. Or, just say the Om mantra. Reciting mantras makes you resolute.'

From the next day, Mother begins reciting mantras.

When Mother does pranayama, we do it too. When she focuses her attention on her navel, on the tip of her nose or a lotus flower, we too try, with eyes closed, to focus our attention like Mother: When I concentrate on my nose, sometimes, my brother's nose comes before my eyes, sometimes Father's or even Panditji's flat nose and, my mind, straying, ends upon a game of gulli-danda.

But Father is never troubled by the problem of concentration. He never even says whether he is able to concentrate during prayers or not. 'Babuji, you are surely able to concentrate while praying?' asks the sadhu. Mother is sitting nearby. Father tilts his head and laughs and says, 'Holy master, we should sit at God's feet twice a day. We should be grateful for that.'

For Father, praying is simply an expression of gratitude, bowing one's head before God and saying thank you for all the things He has given. That is all there is to it. And that can be said in just one minute.

But Mother does not belong only to the Arya Samaj. Sometimes, she puts wheat flour or clarified butter into a small bowl and goes to the Sikh gurudwara. At other times she even goes to a *sanatan dharma* temple. Whenever a child in the house falls ill, Mother certainly goes to a Sikh gurudwara in the morning. And in the evening, she ritually waves chillies around the heads of us two brothers to ward off the evil eye. Occasionally, she observes a fast on the first day of the month. When Mother's friend Goman comes visiting us in the afternoon, she goes with her to the sanatan dharma temple and, when leaving, she says to us, 'Don't tell Father I am going to the shivalay temple. There is a religious discourse on the Bhagwat Gita.'

Whenever there is any reference to us children between Father and Mother, she joins her hands together and says very softly, 'May they remain healthy! May Maharaj keep them safe and sound!'

At this, Father becomes angry.

'What do you mean by saying "Maharaj Maharaj" when we are talking about the children?'

'All right, all right,' Mother says very softly, but her hands remain joined. Whenever there is any mention of us children, she feels apprehensive and is certain to fold her hands and say, 'May they remain in good health.' We can't understand her fears, but we grasp that it has to do with those three children who died one by one, and whose names are sometimes heard around the house. Who they were or what they were like, I don't know.

I only know that one of them was called Saraswati, that her clothes caught fire and that Mother picked her up and threw her into a tub of water. Then, one day, when the doctor was removing her bandages, she let out a shriek and died. The second one was called Shanti. In our house in Peshawar, she was sitting near the balustrade when Mother, thinking that there might be scorpions there, picked her up and seated her close to her beside the staircase. But it was there that a scorpion bit her, and she died on the spot. The third was called Raj and she was only a month old when she died. When Mother folds her hands and says, 'May they remain healthy, may they remain healthy, may Maharaj keep them well,' I imagine the three of them, and I say to myself, if they hadn't died, there would have been seven of us children—five sisters and two brothers.

We would have played in the house the whole day! And Mother would never have uttered these words.

One day there was to be a *havan*, a purification fire, lit in the house. This was because the neighbours, who are *mleccha*, low caste, had roasted a goat's head. Tulsi sprinkled water in the yard near the fence and spread out the prayer mat. From behind the house, wisps of smoke rose and a strange smell was beginning to spread. Mother and my two sisters stood outside the kitchen. My sisters kept wrinkling up their noses.

'They are roasting a goat's head. How wicked! What sinners! The bad smell has spread throughout the neighbourhood.'

'Burning goat's hair smells like that,' said Mother.

'Wicked people roast the goat's head, then eat it. In their next lives, they themselves will become goats and their heads will get roasted.' So said my little sister, angrily shaking her head.

We kept waiting for Father. The havan would be started when he came from downstairs. Actually, Father was not especially interested in havans, for they took up a lot of time. He would say, 'Get started and then I'll come,' and he wouldn't appear. But that day, Mother had already called to him three times from the balustrade. For me, the havan was great fun. The flames from the fire took on all kinds of shapes and seemed to dance in front of my eyes. Sometimes, Mother would pour water into the palm of my hand and tell me to swallow it. I too said 'Om!' all the while watching Mother, and turn by turn placing the tips of my wet fingers on my eyes, nostrils and ears, and sprinkling the last remaining drops of water over my head. I had learned by heart the mantra which had to be recited five times, and I did so in a high-pitched voice along with everyone else.

In his gravelly voice, Tulsi said, 'The smoke from the purified offerings we have put in the sacred fire will put an end to the dirty smoke of those wicked, low-caste people.' Both my sisters giggled.

Father came upstairs, washed his hands and sat down on his prayer mat. Tulsi, who was seated beside the tandoor, started cleaning the globes of the lamps. Mother and Father sat facing each other, and my brother and I sat on one side with our sisters opposite us. First of all, the mantra was repeated, during which Mother added wood to the havan brazier. Next, we drank two or three sips of water, after which, water was sprinkled on each of the four sides of the havan brazier. After the fire was lit, offerings of ghee were made, but only by Father. Everyone else threw *samagri*, herbal preparations, into the fire as an oblation. This seemed very unfair to me.

'Throw in very small quantities,' said my brother, pinching me on the knee, 'otherwise the small bowl will get empty.'

Two or three handfuls of offerings dampened down the flames, and smoke started coming out of the brazier.

My eyes began to smart with the smoke, but I kept sitting there with my eyes wide open. Even when the fire in the brazier became more intense and everyone else began to slide his or her prayer mat farther away, I stuck to my place, because the true Aryan lets the smoke get into his eyes. Then, due to sitting close to the flames, my face became red and, like my brother's red face, began to glow. Otherwise, it was always rather pale.

Fragrant smoke, issuing from the havan brazier, was overcoming the mleccha's smoke. Its fragrance was pervading the whole atmosphere. Tulsi went on cleaning the lamp globes. While the mantras were being recited, Father's voice was the loudest.

After the havan, the prayers started. With folded hands and eyes closed, Father recited a few mantras, then, invoking God, Lord Satchidananda, the Supreme Being, he began praying. We closed our eyes, placed our hands in our laps and bowed our heads.

Father suddenly stopped in the middle of reciting the mantra which preceded the prayer. Silence reigned. Then he started the mantra again.

Again, he broke off. Had he forgotten the mantra? I opened my eyes. Both my sisters too had opened their eyes and were looking in Father's direction. He was still stuck there and wasn't uttering a syllable. My sisters looked quite bewildered. I closed my eyes again.

All of a sudden from the direction of the tandoor, came the sound of Tulsi's loud, gruff voice.

Father had forgotten this part of the mantra. Once he heard it, he started reciting the mantra again and went right through it to the end.

My heart started thumping. I opened my eyes and looked in Tulsi's direction. My younger sister too was looking at him from over her shoulder. He had interrupted. He would surely get a scolding for this.

'Oh God, Satchidananda Swarup, Almighty Father . . .'

The prayer began. With the lamp globe in one hand and a dirty cloth in the other, Tulsi went on with his polishing.

'Oh Dinanath, let there be happiness in this little family, Oh Dayanidhan . . .'

I was still feeling afraid. My brother was sitting, slightly hunched, with his eyes closed. He never ever opened his eyes. Mother too was sitting with an air of deep concentration, like a statue. At the end of the prayer, Father's voice began to quaver: 'Please forgive us for our faults, please forgive us, please forgive us. May you always have mercy on this home, please grant us this, please grant us this, please grant us this . . .'

We all bowed our heads.

'Om Shanti, Shanti, Shanti.' Father opened his eyes and looked at Tulsi. My heart began thumping again. But Father was smiling.

'You are a real bag of virtues, aren't you? Do you know any other mantras?'

Tulsi burbled, 'Yes sir, I know all the mantras.'

'Even the morning, noon and evening prayers?'

'Yes, Father, I know them by heart.'

Mother went on looking fixedly at Father, then said: 'Why wouldn't he, if he has them dinned into him every day?'

Father, still smiling as before, said, 'You may sit with us at havans and prayers. Get up, wash your hands and come here.'

'But, my dear . . .' Mother cut in but stopped.

'Come along now, there's a good lad!'

Tulsi promptly got up, washed his hands and sat in front of the tandoor a little away from Mother's prayer mat.

Before the start of the prayer, Mother once again said, 'Look, all the housework is still to be done . . .' but then, wrinkling her nose and wringing her hands, she fell silent.

The *sandhya* began in a chorus of voices. Tulsi quite unhesitatingly began to recite the mantras in his deep, gruff voice. I opened my eyes just a fraction. My elder sister was stuffing the edge of her dupatta into her mouth to stifle her laughter. And my little sister, to stop herself from laughing, moved a little distance away from her. Seeing my sisters' attempts to prevent themselves from laughing made me want to laugh too, but I quickly closed my eyes and, like my brother, sat immobile.

Tulsi's voice grew louder than before. It was louder even than Father's. He was reciting the mantras of the prayer so fast that Father and Mother were being left behind. Father kept on stopping. I again opened my eyes and had a peep. Father didn't look the slightest bit angry, in fact, he seemed quite delighted. But there was my little sister, still stuffing her dupatta into her mouth. Both my sisters looked at each other for an instant, then quickly turned their heads away. I was frightened.

My sisters wouldn't be able to suppress their laughter—
from just tee-hee-heeing, it would surely burst right out
and Father would be extremely angry. Mother sat there,
looking distracted, and muttered the mantras of the prayer.
Then she fell silent. That day again, Mother found it
difficult to concentrate on the prayer. Tulsi had got ahead
in the recitation of the mantras. Father opened his eyes and
kept looking at Tulsi and smiling. He was very pleased.

When the prayer was over, Father, without saying
anything to anyone, began singing a hymn and clapping
his hands:

> *God provides for all of His innumerable*
> *creatures according to their needs . . .*

In this too, Tulsi's voice was mingled. Father's high-
pitched, inharmonious voice and Tulsi Ram's deep gruff
voice began to vie with each other. Father kept up his
gentle clapping, and at times his head would lean over to
one side . . .

The moment Tulsi had begun singing, both my sisters
erupted into laughter and rolled about together on the
ground, making vain attempts to cram their dupattas into
their mouths.

Suddenly, Mother too started laughing. Whenever
Mother laughed, her stomach would start wobbling. She
laughed only for a moment, her whole body shaking, then
she fell silent and sat as still as a statue. After some time,
her body started shaking again.

'Vidya, Vimla!' scolded Father, raising his voice. Both sisters kept quiet, but only for a second. Just looking at Tulsi, who was singing with head held high, they completely lost control. Once again they burst into laughter, then both of them got up and ran off.

After the hymn, came the prayer beseeching God for peace. Tulsi had committed this too to memory. But the moment the prayer ended, Mother put her hands on her knees and stood up. 'Vidya, Vimla! Pick up the mats and put them on the chhajja. Be quick. It's getting late.'

Even then, Father kept on looking at Tulsi and smiling. 'From tomorrow, sit with us every day.'

'Yes, sit with us every day!' interjected Mother. 'What am I for? Only to be the household drudge? Come on now, get up, Tulsi. The prayers are over. Get up and light the stove. Don't you see what time it is?'

After Tulsi had left, Father said to Mother in a low voice, 'That boy is intelligent. If he joins in our prayers and havans, he will become a man. He must have lived somewhere among orthodox Brahmins. You shouldn't interfere in everything.'

'Oh, I beg your pardon. My mistake. Go ahead and make him an Arya Samajist and sadhu. What has it got to do with me? He was always a lazybones. And now, if you give him big ideas about himself, he won't do any work at all.'

And Mother turned and went off to the kitchen. Then Father said to Baldev, who was sitting close by, 'From tomorrow, when your tutor comes, make Tulsi sit with you. And get him a copy book and pen also.' My brother replied that he did sit with them and could write as well as read Hindi.

At night, the kitchen work over, Mother put the starter in the milk to set the curds. Tulsi sat in a corner of the kitchen, cleaning utensils. Lying on our cots, we brothers kept hearing the clatter of utensils until late. After scouring and cleaning them, Tulsi washed out the kitchen, and while he did so, Mother and Father went and sat in the sitting room which had a clock in it.

Mother usually sat cross-legged on the bed, while Father sauntered up and down the room with his hands behind his back. This was almost a daily ritual. Sitting there, Mother would sometimes de-husk melon seeds, and at other times would tell her beads. While she was busy with her rosary, there was no prohibition on speaking. We would hear snatches of their conversation. Sometimes, all of a sudden, they would start quarrelling and, as things deteriorated, their voices too would rise. Then Mother would get up, muttering, and come into our room, while Father went on striding up and down in the sitting room until late at night.

'Now you are treating him like one of us,' said Mother. 'You are bent upon ruining his life.'

Father stopped in mid-stride and said, 'Will becoming literate ruin his life? Have you taken leave of your senses?'

'If he reads and writes, what will he do? Will he become a bank manager? All he will do is clean utensils, what else? Let him be as he is. Why ruin his life?'

'All right, that's enough, I've got the point. But don't keep lecturing me all the time.'

Father started walking up and down again.

'You people go about converting people to the Arya Samaj. Why don't you deal first with the ones you have already converted? There was that Muslim you "purified" wasn't there? The people from the Arya Samaj never tired of talking about him. It was, "Arjan Dev this and Arjan Dev that." You were even going to arrange his marriage. Nanak Chand came and said to me, "Mataji, please give me some bedsheets. Arjan Dev is going to do printing work." He took a total of four brand new bedsheets from me. Now where has Arjan Dev gone? After taking sheets and clothes from dozens of people, he has simply vanished.'

'Go on, talk. Say whatever comes into your head. Don't stop. If Tulsi does a little reading, how will that harm anyone?'

Lying in bed. I felt afraid the quarrel would get worse and both of them would start raising their voices. Mother would say, 'What happiness have I had with you? You've always caused me unhappiness.' And if the quarrel became even worse, she would join her hands and sob, 'Oh Lord, take me away, take me to where my Saraswati, my Shanti, and my Raj have gone.' But the quarrel didn't get worse. Mother only went on fretting, saying, 'What is it to me? Go on and teach him, make him an Arya Samajist. He will end up fitting in nowhere.' Then the conversation took another turn. They started talking about something quite different. Perhaps somebody was getting engaged. Maybe, a letter had come from somewhere. My sister Vidya's name too kept getting mentioned. Was she getting engaged? What did 'engaged' mean? Gradually their voices became more and more indistinct.

§

Mother's keys had got lost again. This was a daily occurrence. Mother got up from the churn in which she had whipped up the curds and began to look for them among the innumerable folds of her salwar. Suddenly, from some far-off spot, the sound of somebody sneezing was heard. It was the sweetmeat maker Attar Singh sneezing.

'Look now, Attar Singh has sneezed, but not a single bit of kitchen work has been done yet.'

The daily routine for many of the people in our neighbourhood was tied up with the sweetmeat maker Attar Singh's sneeze. He would always sneeze at exactly eleven o'clock. To see the response to it, I would run up to the chhajja. Opposite our house, Fez Ali, hearing the sneeze, would leave aside his hookah, get up from his cot and, passing his hand across his face, would say, 'Time to be off!' and he would start hitching his horse to his tonga.

From the left, Maulvi Ishaq would come out of his house with his rosary in hand and start off down the middle of the street in the direction of the mosque to say the eleven o'clock prayer.

Father would call up from the yard below, 'Baldev's mother! Have you sent milk to the school for the children? Where on earth is Tulsi?'

Vidya would come running to the balustrade. 'What is it, Father?'

'Attar Singh has sneezed and you people still haven't sent milk to the children? Where is Tulsi?'

'Today they both have a holiday, Father, it's the festival of the full moon,' said Vidya, laughing.

Father stood there for a moment without saying anything, then, 'So, why didn't you say so before?' And with that, he went into his office.

Mother would take the butter out of the churn at Attar Singh's very first sneeze. But that day, the missing keys had created a problem. Mother was stout in build and it seemed to me that it couldn't be from anywhere else but the folds of her clothes that the bunch of keys would come clinking out.

'I gave them just now to Vidya after taking out the ghee. Come now, Vidya, where are the keys? How is it that everyone seems struck dumb?'

Vidya came running from the old sufa.

'I gave them to you, Mother.'

Mother came out of the kitchen and across to the balustrade. 'Baldev's father, have you by any chance seen the keys?'

The sound of a chair scraping on the floor came to us from downstairs, then a moment later, Father called out from the yard below, 'If I've told you once, I've told you a thousand times—keep them tied to a corner of your dupatta. How would I know where they are? Have you looked in the painter's cupboard?' Whenever anything got lost, we always rummaged about for it in the painter's cupboard.

Mother came back from the balustrade. She was becoming more and more perplexed and irritated. She started searching around the butter churn again and her hand went into the folds of her salwar once more. 'If they had been here, wouldn't I have found them? This house is so untidy that if anything goes a-missing, everybody seems to be deliberately acting dumb about it.'

We four—brothers and sisters—started looking for the keys. In the painter's cupboard, on the kitchen stove, in the box room (in which the ghee was also kept), in the lamp niche, behind the open cooking fire, underneath the prayer mats. The keys were not to be found anywhere.

'Have you found the keys?' Father's voice could be heard again from downstairs.

'No, Father, not yet,' answered Vidya from the balustrade. Father's heavy tread could be heard on the stairs.

'I gave them just now to Vidya after taking out the ghee. Vidya, why are you sitting there and just not saying anything? Why don't you say something?'

And Mother went to the kitchen stove and, standing on tiptoe, started looking for the keys.

'You'll never find them like this.' Father had left his work and come upstairs. Mother was still moving here and there in a state of anxiety. Father suggested that she sit down in one place, close her eyes and try to remember where she had last seen them. 'The bunch of keys will certainly not appear all by itself.'

'Much good that will do! I just gave it to Vidya after taking the ghee out.'

When, despite everything, Mother couldn't remember, she actually did sit down, close her eyes and try to think of the various places where the keys had been used.

'I took out money to give to the vegetable seller.'

'It was I who gave him the money,' Father cut in. 'You're thinking about what happened yesterday. Now try again to remember.'

Then we heard a very light step on the stairs. Only our youngest aunt, my mother's sister, stepped so softly. Whenever she came to the house, we four children would crowd around her. She was very small and shapely, and kept smiling gently all the time.

'Maasi has come,' said Vidya, looking through the peephole. Then, calling through the peephole, she said, 'Maasiji, our keys have got lost. We've been looking for them all morning.' Maasi came in, having taken off her shoes as she set foot in the courtyard.

'I've been searching for them all morning and now I have to give up,' said Mother.

'Why don't we ask the astrologer? He's sitting right here by the ditch,' said Maasi. 'Shall I go and ask him? He takes only one paisa. I'll go and ask.'

And Maasi, retracing her steps, started to put on her shoes.

'What will the astrologer do?' asked Father, irritated.

'What is the harm in asking, my dear brother, he's only going to take one paisa.' And Maasi set off down the staircase.

'Do as you please,' said Father, becoming even more irritated. Being an Arya Samajist, he abhorred astrologers.

Maasi called through the peephole in the staircase.

'You should also put the question to the Ramayana—by putting one's finger at random on the chart of letters provided in the Ramayana, one can, in accordance with a formula, decipher the message—and see what it says. Sometimes it turns out to be right.' And she went downstairs.

'Let it be, sister, what is the point in doing things which are displeasing to the menfolk?'

'Unless she has one particular place for the keys, they will keep on getting lost every day,' said Father. 'See, now, I'll fix a place for you to put them in future.' And he walked over to the painter's cupboard.

'There was a hammer lying here. Where has it gone?' Father kept moving boxes and empty bottles around inside the painter's cupboard, in his search for it. 'In this house, nothing can ever be found in its place.'

'The hammer must be somewhere downstairs, my dear. What use is there for a hammer here?' asked Mother, sitting down by her butter churn.

'Where has Tulsi gone to? He must have put it somewhere,' muttered Father. Finally, he took a long nail out of the painter's cupboard and, picking up a brick from a pile of bricks near the staircase, he went over to the new sufa and hammered the nail into a wall. 'Now,' he said, 'everybody, pay attention! Let the keys be hung here. Whenever you remove them, hang them back in this very spot after using them.'

It wasn't just for keys that Father kept making fixed places, but for other things too. The lamp had to be kept in a particular niche and whoever took it away had to bring it back and put it right back there. The funnel for pouring oil had to be kept in the neck of the bottle. Once before, when the keys had got lost, Father himself had tied them on to the end of Mother's dupatta, and we children stood around and kept laughing, because very seldom did we see Father and Mother being playful with each other.

After fixing a place for the keys, Father stood in front of the new sufa and looked at the clock on the wall, which had stopped several days before. 'All right, I'd better get this started too.'

Father stood up on a stool and wound the clock; then, by moving the hands around, he made it chime nine times, ten times, eleven times. Having pointed the hands to eleven fifteen, he closed the glass door of the clock face. Then he took a pencil out of his shirt pocket and drew lines outlining the framework of the clock.

'Now, Baldev's mother, just understand this. Nobody is to move the clock. The clock is to stay within these lines.'

Apart from Father, nobody moved the clock. To reach up to it, he himself had to climb up on a stool. But every time he wound the clock, he would give everybody these instructions. Then, with the same pencil, he wrote beside the clock in Urdu, 'Wind on Tuesday.'

And then he scored out 'Wind on Saturday' which was written above it. Two other lines of writing had already been scored out above this. Stepping down from the stool, he said, 'These are small things, but they still need to be attended to.'

Maasi had come back and, going over to Mother, she told her with much whispering that the astrologer had said that the keys were in the dark room, five paces to the right.

'That is the very room which has a lock on it,' said Mother in despair.

'It could also be the room where the straw is kept,' babbled Vidya. 'You did go there. Didn't you go to let out the cow? But I'm not going to look there,' she quickly added, 'I might get bitten by a scorpion or something.'

'No, why should you go? We'll send Tulsi.' But Mother doesn't believe that the keys could be there. 'Good heavens, girl, I gave them to you later on, after I had taken out the ghee.'

'Look in the kitchen, sister, it's dark in there too,' said Maasi.

Vimla came and stood silently in the doorway, with both her hands behind her back. She was smiling just a little. Vidya was the first to notice her. 'Have the keys been found?' she shouted, leaping across to her. Why wasn't Vimla singing out? If Vidya had found the keys, she would have been jumping about, rattling them and saying, 'I've found the keys. I've found the keys!' She would have been raising the roof. But my little sister only kept smiling a little with her head tilted to one side. She talked and laughed very little.

'My goodness, child, where did you find them?' asked Mother, coming away from the balustrade. Vexed and worried, she kept wiping her face with her dupatta.

'They were underneath the butter churn.'

'Didn't I say so?' said Mother, clapping her hands. 'If they were anywhere, it would be near the churn. They couldn't go away anywhere. I generally sit right here. I gave them to Vidya after taking out the ghee and she must have put them there. For my part, I never let the keys out of my sight.'

'Father, Father! The keys have been found!'

The chair in the office could again be heard scraping on the floor, and Father came out into the courtyard. 'Now tell Mother to hang them on the nail.' Then, seeing Mother standing by the balustrade, he said, 'Baldev's mother, if you have any curds, send me a little in a *katori*, bowl, and I'll just go and have a bath.'

Mother at once turned back and said, looking down, 'If you have a bath now, when will you have your milk? Look how late in the morning it is and you still haven't had your milk. Then you say there's no order in this house.'

'My good lady, why are you arguing? Does it take hours to have a bath? I could have had a bath in the time it has taken you to give me this lecture.'

At this Mother shook her head, and, in a sing-song voice, recited:

The maulvi, the preacher and the torch-bearer
are alike.
They lighten others' paths, but walk in
darkness themselves.

Then she moved away from the balustrade.

∽

In the afternoon, the noise started up again in our street. Mother was sitting with both my sisters, stitching clothes on the sewing machine. The moment she heard the noise her face turned pale: 'They are robbing some hawker again today. The good-for-nothings!'

Both my sisters ran over to the window and started peeping down through the *chick*, the reed sunshade.

I know what must have happened. Around four o'clock, when our Panditji was leaving after our lesson, and the shadows in our street were beginning to lengthen, a hawker carrying a trayful of samosas on his shoulder would turn into our locality from the direction of the manger. He was an elderly man with a fair complexion. Nobody tried any tricks with him. But sometimes, when his son or some other man brought the tray, he would be made to sit down in front of the sheikh's son, Maulvi Ishaq's son and Lamboo—all from our street—and then the three of them would gorge themselves on samosas and *kachori*s, but when he asked for payment, they would start to beat him.

Then Father would go outside, save the hawker from being beaten up, and, really raising his voice, would reprimand Maulvi Ishaq's son. All the while, Mother's heart would be thumping. She would run from the balustrade to the window.

Today again, there was a noise coming from downstairs. The sheikh's son and his cronies must be looting the wares of some hawker.

'But there's nobody down there in the lane, Mother,' said Vidya, turning around.

'So they must be in the street,' said Mother, and immediately got up and went to the chhajja.

A man was tied to a pole in front of our house. Fez Ali had taken off his turban and was using it to leash the man really tightly to the pole. He kept pulling the ends of the turban to make it even tighter. The man was bent over double in front. His face had become red and his eyes were protruding. There was nothing he could do to free himself because his hands were tied behind his back. Whenever he leant so far forward that it hindered his being tied up, Fez Ali punched him so hard in the face that his head shot back, then rolled on to his shoulders. Blood had started flowing from his lips. I felt as if my knees had turned to water and my legs had started trembling.

Baba Noora came hobbling out of his *kothari*, went straight to the pole and began belabouring the tied-up man with his stick. People started collecting.

'Oh God, the butcher will kill him, he'll finish him off,' said Mother, in a state of great trepidation.

She suddenly left the chhajja and rushed down to Father's office. My brother, sisters and I stayed by the balustrade. Father had come out of his office and was on his way to the courtyard when Mother stopped him.

'If you go out, it will be over my dead body. You go about making enemies with everybody in the neighbourhood. It's not a good thing.'

'If we are to live in the neighbourhood, is it to be like frightened little mice?'

'If you go out, it will be over my dead body. I swear by my little children that it will be so if you set foot outside the house. I am falling at your feet.'

'What nonsense is this!' Freeing his feet from Mother's grasp, Father went towards the street. My brother and I came downstairs.

'Where is Tulsi?' asked Mother, raising her head. 'Vidya, Vimla, just see where Tulsi is. Don't let him come downstairs.'

'Tulsi is asleep on the chhajja.'

'Don't let him come downstairs.'

Father went out of the house.

'Oh Lord! Give him some sense! He goes about creating complications with everyone.'

Father reached the pole. He wasn't wearing his turban. Without it, he looked very frail. We two brothers went back into the house and up on the terrace. I stared at the man tied to the pole. He was fair-skinned and had a brown beard which was stained on one side with blood.

Father said something very quietly to Baba Noora. Fez Ali was still trussing up the man even more tightly, but Baba Noora had stopped wielding his stick.

'Look, Babu, you've no idea what all this is about. This son of a bitch has come from some other locality.' And he again began thrashing the man on the shoulders with his stick, and saying something in a loud voice which I didn't understand.

Fez Ali reached into the pocket of the man's jacket, which was hanging open, pulled out a bottle and showed it to Father. There was a small quantity of yellow liquid in it. And seeing that, more blows from Noora's stick rained down on the man.

Father talked to them very quietly. Whenever a hawker was robbed, he talked in a very loud voice. But now, standing there, he was reasoning with Baba Noora and Fez Ali. Fez Ali's efforts were now slackening, even if now and then he punched the man so that his head swung from right to left.

Now, Father came back. Once across the courtyard, he turned straight into his office. He was unhitching the chain on the office door. In the meantime, Mother, who had gone upstairs—perhaps to see everything from the chhajja, or to keep Tulsi from going out—reached the balustrade.

'Now will you just tell me what happened?'

'Nothing. Nothing at all.'

'Whatever you might say, something did happen. A man was tied to a pole and beaten.'

'He isn't one of their lot. He was sitting here in some small room, drinking liquor and . . .' Then, seeing us standing there, he fell silent and went inside.

We rushed back up on to the chhajja, because we could hear a noise coming again from the same place. A number of *lathi*-wielding men, cursing loudly, came running from the direction of the manger. Fez Ali ran to his room and brought out a shovel. Karam Khan's son and Fateh Din picked up lathis from their rooms and arrived at the pole. Three of the men from the manger attacked Fez Ali and Baba Noora. Fez Ali stepped forward and gave one of the men a severe blow with the shovel, cutting his jaw; blood came gushing out. Blood was flowing from Baba Noora's head too. Somebody started freeing the trussed-up man. From the neighbouring lane, the subedar's nephew arrived carrying a hockey stick, with which he hit one of the men in the back really hard. Many of the local residents had come out and in loud voices were making attempts to put an end to the fight. Attar Singh, the sweetmeat maker, was among them. His turban could be seen, bobbing up now in one place, now in another. Two more lathi-wielding men came running from the manger, with two women right behind them. One of the women was carrying her shoes in her hand.

Now, in the crowd, the man who was tied to the pole couldn't be seen. Fewer lathis were being brandished. And Mother pulled us away from the chhajja.

Downstairs, Father had started work in the office again. What work he did, I didn't know. He sat in the office and typed letters with one finger. Thursday was his foreign mail day, and he would sit in the office the whole day. Then nobody could call him, not even Mother. He gave Mother cloth samples which she would use for making kurtas and pyjamas for us, after my sisters had removed the pictures. There was a large box in which there were innumerable pencils. There were also bowls of many different colours, on a few of which there were words written in English, like, 'Remember me!' 'Forget me not!' etc. Traders would come to the house and Father would sit in the office and go on talking to them.

'Tulsi!' It was Father calling up from the courtyard. I ran to the balustrade. Father was standing in the courtyard and, right behind him, there were two men, one of whom was wearing a fez. The other had on a silk turban and his legs were clothed in a really wide salwar. Both were Muslims. I ran to Mother in the sitting room where she had sat down again at the sewing machine to stitch clothes.

'Mother, there are two Muslims downstairs.' Mother first glanced at me in surprise, then she quietly got up and went over to the balustrade. Tulsi came running from the chhajja, rubbing his eyes, and made straight for the staircase. In the meantime, Father had gone back into the office and closed the door from inside. Standing at the balustrade, Mother bent over slightly in an attempt to hear what kind of sounds were coming from inside. But not a single sound could be heard. Mother moved away and was on the point of going back to her sewing machine when Tulsi came rushing upstairs.

'Mother, two traders have come and Father says to send something for them to eat.'

'Go light the fire and put on water for tea,' said Mother, going off to the kitchen. Outside the kitchen, in a niche, were kept two china plates, two cups with a floral pattern, and a kind of teapot. We never ate or drank anything from them. They always lay there. They were for the Muslim traders who were given tea and something to eat. And after they went away, Mother would clean these tea things with burning embers and hot ash, and put them back in the niche.

Knowing that these men were just traders and had not come to quarrel with Father, I plucked up courage and went downstairs. I quietly opened the office door and went inside.

Father was sitting on a long leather bench and holding a shiny length of thread in his hand.

'Six and a quarter per bobbin, Khan Sahib. I can't reduce it any further. How many boxes should I write?'

'The price is too high,' said the turbaned Muslim.

'Not for you, Khan Sahib,' said Father extending his hand and touching him under the chin. 'This kind of thread just isn't made anymore. It used to be made by a firm in France. All the other manufacturers were ruined in the war.'

'The price is too high,' repeated the turbaned Muslim.

'How many boxes should I write? Don't give it too much thought, Khan Sahib. In the whole of Peshawar, I do not supply the thread to anyone but you. All right then, we'll have a compromise—six per bobbin. It can't be less than that. I'm making no profit on this, Khan Sahib, I swear to you.'

There was a big difference between these Muslim businessmen and the Muslims of our neighbourhood. Father talked laughingly with the former and chucked them under the chin. He gave them tea and things to eat. But the local Muslims were mlechhas. They roasted goats' heads, they robbed Hindu hawkers, their children sang bawdy songs and used filthy language. For that reason, Father wouldn't let us play with them.

Tulsi started bringing in the snacks.

Father told me to go upstairs. I did so and went directly on to the chhajja. On the street, the crowd had thinned out. Two men were lying on cots, with white sheets draped over them. Policemen were moving here and there. The woman who had been carrying her shoes in her hand sat beside one of the cots, weeping and ceaselessly beating her hand on the support. For a long time I stayed on the chhajja. Much later, the cots were lifted up and taken out of our neighbourhood with a few people walking close behind them.

My brother and I came down. Both my sisters stood at the balustrade and looked down into the courtyard. Downstairs, Tulsi was standing in front of Father. He had put on a turban, and was wearing an old overcoat of Father's. Since he had started sitting with us to study, he always put on a turban when he had to go out. He never went out bareheaded.

'You fool! You've brought it back! If you had mentioned my name to the clerk, he would have taken it.'

'I use your name every day, but he didn't take it this time. The mail bag had already been closed.'

I understood what it was all about. Almost every evening, Father scolded Tulsi about the letters. The post box nearest to our house was the one next to Attar Singh's sweetmeat shop. It was quite close by. From there, the mail was collected before sundown.

Farther ahead, beyond the crossing, was the post office, from where the mail was collected at five thirty, after the sun had gone down, but before it had got really dark. Then there was the main post office in town in the Talwaranwala Bazaar, which was very far from our house. There, the mail was collected at seven o'clock, just as it got dark. And if it got later than that, the letters could be posted at the railway station, on the train leaving at 10 p.m. Tulsi generally went to post the letters at the main post office, where the collection time was seven o'clock. That day, he had brought the letters back.

'You good-for-nothing fellow! All you can do is gobble food. Now why are you gaping at me? Be off with you, quickly, to the railway station. Go directly, across the town nullah, post the letters and come straight back.'

'Nothing in this house is normal,' said Mother, who had come out of the kitchen to the balustrade. 'The post box is only two steps away from the house. If you could just write the letters earlier, the work would be done right away. Now when will Tulsi come back? All the housework is still to be done.'

'You see to your own work, my dear lady. Why do you interfere?'

'You lecture to the family about punctuality . . .' said Mother, standing at the balustrade. Father went straight into the living room and went on muttering there.

Hearing Father's mutterings made all our hearts miss a beat. Now the quarrel would get worse. My little sister quietly went and stood beside Mother. She pulled the end of her dupatta and said, 'Let him talk, but don't you say anything, Mother.'

'What was wrong with my saying that whatever he wanted to send should be sent at the proper time? Tulsi has to go every day to the railway station to post the letters.'

'Enough, Mother, don't you say anything,' whispered Vimla again, pulling the end of Mother's dupatta.

Father crossed the living room and went into the small back room.

'What are you people about? Look at the time! The lamp hasn't been lit yet.'

'Go and light the lamp, Vidya,' said Mother. 'When it is time for the housework to be done, you send Tulsi out to post letters.'

Infuriated, Father said, 'So, now the office work is to be done only with your leave!'

Wearily, Mother turned away from the balustrade. 'Do whatever you want. What joy in life have I ever had before that I should have any now?'

'I'm leaving, I'm leaving. Since I've given you no joy, I'll relieve you of my presence.'

And Father started going down the stairs. On the stairs, too, he muttered, 'I've given her no happiness!'

Mother went and sat down in the kitchen. Her face remained red with vexation. We children crouched close around her in fear. A great silence and a great heaviness had descended upon the house. Holding on to the end of Mother's dupatta, Baldev asked piteously if Father wouldn't come back home. She said she didn't know and looked away.

Baldev started crying: 'Father has gone away, now he won't come back.' His sobbing grew louder. Mother stared at my brother, but didn't utter a word. My little sister, Vimla, got up and came over to Baldev and wiped away his tears with her dupatta. 'Don't cry, don't cry, my dear brother, please don't cry,' she said, then started crying herself. And the four of us began to sob.

Slapping her own hands, Mother said, 'I'm a wretch. I've no control over my tongue. I keep on chattering . . .' Then she joined her hands, 'Oh God, please make me more sensible. I blurt out whatever comes into my mouth.' Suddenly, pushing her mat back, she leaned against the wall and said, 'From today I'll observe a vow of silence. That's it. Now I won't speak.'

As a result of her agitation, her features were still suffused with red. We were all familiar with Mother's periods of silence. Every fifth or sixth day, Mother would pledge herself to remaining silent and, without speaking, she would quietly set about doing the housework. She would get small jobs done by Vimla and Vidya by making

signs to them. That day, as always, Vimla brought a slate
and pencil, for Mother had to make herself understood by
writing.

The atmosphere in the house became even more
oppressive than before. Tulsi still hadn't come back. The
cooking fire was slowly going out. Vidya had lit only one
lamp, the one which was kept in the niche by the staircase.

'Mother, shall I light the tandoor?' asked Vidya.

Mother said nothing at first, then she shook her head.
Vidya didn't understand what this meant.

'Shall I light it or not? Or will Tulsi come and light it?'

Mother again shook her head. My sisters looked at
each other. Then both of them sat with their chins on
their knees, staring at the floor without saying a word. Just
then, a voice came from below. 'Are you listening?' It was
Father's voice. 'Are you listening?'

'Baldev's mother! The calf has drunk up the milk.
When that fellow Tulsi goes off, he doesn't even think
about coming back.'

Baldev sprang up and went to the balustrade.

'You've come back, Father?'

'I haven't even started out yet. Tell Mother that I've
tied up the calf now. No great damage has been done. I'll
be back shortly.'

Then the sound of the door closing could be heard.
We started chattering again. Baldev, standing behind
Mother and clutching her shoulder, kept saying, 'Please,
Mother, break your vow of silence. Father won't go away
anywhere now.'

We all urged her. Mother wasn't unbending.

And, after a little while, with a deep sigh, she broke her silence and said, 'Oh, well then, I have to answer for my deeds, and he for his.' Then she got up and started re-lighting the fire. It was getting dark.

Today, after the meal, Mother didn't go into Father's room to chat. Father sauntered up and down in the sitting room as he did every day. Mother, who was sitting on her cot in the darkness, suddenly began to sing:

> *Never lose your fear of the Almighty,*
> *For the Almighty does as He wills.*

In between, the sounds of Father's footsteps could be heard.

> *In a split second the raja is on his throne,*
> *And in a split second he may be gone.*

On any other day, Father would have scolded her, for he didn't like songs of that kind. He called them joyless. But that day he remained silent, and kept quietly pacing up and down. Tulsi finished his work in the kitchen and went up to sleep on the chhajja. All the lamps were put out. The house was pitch-dark. Mother went on singing:

> *Never lose your fear of the Almighty,*
> *For the Almighty does as He wills . . .*

'You are Chetak (Rana Pratap's famous horse). Shake your head like this and this. I'm going to leap on to your back.' We were in the pantry and my brother was telling me to run into the corner.

The pantry door opened into the old sufa but, for the time being, it had been closed. 'Go round from the back and bring elder sister's dupatta.'

'What for?'

'Rana Pratap used to wear a turban—haven't you seen the picture? Go on, hurry up and bring it.'

I jumped over from the chhajja into the old sufa, where the spectators of the drama—my little sister, my big sister and a friend of theirs, Manorama—were sitting in front of the closed pantry door. The first roll of the drum had been sounded, so I promptly pulled the dupatta from my sister's head and dashed back to the chhajja. My sister shrieked, then started to laugh.

I looked transfixed at my brother's face. Using ink made from powdered charcoal, he had made himself a moustache, from one end of which a drop was sliding down towards his chin. But my brother would soon set that right. There wasn't anything that my brother couldn't do.

'Tulsi! Give us the second roll of the drum.'

Sitting on the chhajja, Tulsi beat on a tin can. It had been decided to use the chhajja for the drumming, so that the whole neighbourhood could be informed about the performance of the play.

My brother wound the turban around his head. Then he fixed a royal plume into it—a feather dropped by a parrot—while I thrust a cardboard sword into his waistband.

'Don't forget to toss your head—like this—horses toss their heads like this,' said my brother.

Suddenly a voice was heard from below, 'Tulsi!' It was Father's voice. 'Tulsi! Come downstairs and pick up the luggage.'

Leaving off the drumming, Tulsi ran by way of the bathroom to the staircase. Both my sisters ran out from behind the closed door in the old sufa and reached the chhajja. Rana Pratap and Chetak looked at each other. 'Somebody has come to visit.'

The two of us ran on to the chhajja. A bus had stopped in front of the house. A man with a thick coating of dust on his head and face was standing below, holding a trunk which was handed over to Tulsi Ram. There were five people standing beside the bus.

'Our sisters have come from Kashmir,' shouted Vidya and both my sisters ran downstairs. We two brothers also went down at a gallop.

Bending down and hugging me, a lady said, 'My goodness, don't you give him anything to eat, dear brother? Just see how thin he's getting!' Then she kissed me over and over again. For the first time, I caught a whiff of a new odour, which came perhaps from that lady's warm clothes. It was the fragrance of the clothes worn by people coming from Kashmir. A tall man was embracing Father. Both the men were wearing very large turbans. Do even such grown-up people embrace each other? Behind the lady stood three girls wearing long warm coats. One was wearing glasses, gold-framed glasses. Looking at my brother, the three sisters laughed. He still had our sister's dupatta around his head, and the black ink from his moustache had by now spread all over his chin. A fair-skinned boy, much bigger than my brother, was getting luggage unloaded piece by piece and handing it over to Tulsi.

Had these people come from beyond the mountain that we could see from the roof? We went into the old sitting room, where the young man was tightening the cords of a bed. He was the brother of these three sisters. He put one foot on the leg of the bed, then, with his tongue sticking out between compressed lips, he used both hands to pull the rope. As he pulled, his face became red, like those of real celibates. We two brothers stared at him without blinking. The three sisters from Kashmir were sitting on the nearby bed. Our two sisters also sat on the same bed.

Tulsi brought glasses of steaming hot tea on a tray.

'In Kashmir we have our tea with salt,' said the girl wearing glasses.

My brother, standing by the fire, was giving his rapt attention to the boy who was tightening the bed strings. I was sitting bashfully on the edge of another bed.

'What rubbish!' I blurted out. 'There's no such thing as salty tea.'

'Of course there is, you silly ass. Kashmiris definitely put salt in their tea.'

I was even more surprised than before.

'We also eat *bakarkhani*, sweetish unleavened bread, there,' said the youngest girl. When she got off the bus, her face had been red, now it had become pale, but her teeth really gleamed.

'Have you ever eaten bakarkhani?' she asked me.

I shook my head.

What different world had these people come from? Never before had I heard such talk or such names for things. Nor had I ever seen such clothes or smelt the kind of scents coming from them. Were these people fairies?

Refusing to accept their superiority, I immediately came out with, 'I know all the prayers.'

'So do I,' she said, laughing. 'Do you know the sacred stanzas?'

'What is a sacred stanza?' I asked, feeling put to shame.

'What! He doesn't even know what a sacred stanza is, the nitwit!' she said to her sisters, laughing. All the sisters turned round and looked at me.

'Come on, let's recite the sacred stanzas,' said the sister wearing glasses, and the three sisters sat cross-legged on the bed.

'Oh, it's very hot here,' said her sister—the broad-faced one with curly hair—taking off her shawl. 'There, we keep sitting in front of a *bukhari* (a small brazier) all the time.'

'What's a bukhari?' I wondered. Again, I felt embarrassed and inferior. What were bakarkhanis? What was a nitwit? I stared wide-eyed at them. The three sisters, sitting cross-legged, began reciting the stanzas.

Their brother too came and sat on the bed which was next to them and recited the stanzas along with them.

These were Kashmiri stanzas, I thought, like Kashmiri bakarkhanis and salty tea. They'd brought them from Kashmir.

Tulsi was still standing in the doorway, listening to the Kashmiri stanzas. During the recitation, they did not close their eyes and, in between, they even talked to each other and let their legs dangle from the bed.

'He too knows the mantras,' said my elder sister, pointing to Tulsi.

'He can also read. He can read the entire primer,' said my little sister proudly. If they had their bakarkhanis and their stanzas, we had our Tulsi to show them.

'He knows hymns too,' she went on, 'I taught him a hymn.'

'Let's hear it then. Which hymn does he know?'

'We only sing hymns in praise of God, nothing else.'

'What's all this?' snapped Mother. 'Fun and games? Haven't you any work to do?' Standing in the doorway, arms akimbo, she scolded Tulsi. 'If only there was some set routine in this house! Here I am, killing myself in the kitchen! And does anybody care? Get along with you! Now what are you standing there staring at me for?'

Discouraged, Tulsi bowed his head and left the room without a word.

Mother returned to the kitchen, grumbling audibly.

The girl with the curly hair said to her sisters: 'You too go and get the work done along with Mamiji.' Bewildered, everyone got up one by one.

The next day we all paired off age-wise. My sisters showed the eldest girl the cupboard where their books were kept. Baldev talked to the girl with glasses about games with bows and arrows.

'From a lying-down position I can shoot an arrow with my big toe. And I can take aim by looking into a mirror the way Arjun used to do.'

'Do you stage plays?' she asked.

'Of course we do. We put on plays about Prithviraj Chauhan, about Shravan Kumar, about Rana Pratap. We were acting yesterday too. My brother was doing the part of Chetak, the horse, and I was Rana Pratap.'

'Have you got a crown?'

Abashed, my brother said, 'I just put on a turban.'

'All right, tomorrow I'll make you a crown.'

The youngest girl was sitting on the bed with her back against the wall. She was reading a big book. I crept over to her and stood beside the bed, staring fixedly at her. Under my gaze, her face, which had been pale, flushed red. She raised her eyes from her book and looked at me. Then she closed the book and started to chat. 'Do you know, our Panditaniji knows all the four Vedas.' So saying, she tightened her lips and shook her head. Then she whispered, 'And do you know, her husband is blind in one eye.' She again tightened her lips and shook her head. 'He used to worship idols in secret, that's how he became blind.'

All along I had been looking at her gleaming teeth.

'Are your teeth made of pearls?' I asked her.

For a split second she looked at me, then she laughed.

'Nitwit, pearls are for making necklaces. Could they ever be made into teeth?' And she grasped my finger and ran it over her teeth.

I said very softly, 'Our Panditji says it's a sin to look at a woman's face. But you're not a woman, you're a girl.'

She shook her head.

'Our Panditji too is a great sinner. He committed some sins for which his nose got flattened.'

As I said this, I tried to imitate the way she tightened her lips and shook her head.

Voices could be heard coming from the courtyard. Both my sisters had moved away from the cupboard. Standing in the doorway, they were looking out on to the courtyard.

Our big brother from Kashmir had picked up a skipping rope and was running and jumping with it across the whole width of the courtyard. Now, retracing his steps, he was running and jumping back again. He was a real hero. He could do the greatest of deeds. His top-knot was longer than ours and was knotted in the true manner of the religious celibate. I envied him his plait. As he ran, it bobbed up and down, while our plaits—mine and my brother's—stayed limp around our ears. Just last night, seeing his plait, I had tied a knot in my trim little plait, which made it even shorter.

Now he had stopped skipping with the rope. His two sisters came into the courtyard and sat down on the ground facing each other. Then they stretched their legs right out, putting their feet together. Our champion came running up and, with one leap, sailed right over their legs. For a long time he went on doing various stunts.

In between, he would catch hold of my brother's wrist. My brother would twist from one side to the other to free himself, but to no avail. However, when my brother caught hold of his wrist, he would free himself with just one quick movement. When they were done playing, I slipped across to him and asked in an undertone, 'Have you seen God?' I was convinced that if anyone in this world had seen God, he would be the person.

He looked at me in surprise, then, very quietly, and with perfect self-assurance, he said: 'I did see Him once.'

I gazed at him wonderstruck.

'One day when I was saying my prayers, my whole vision was filled with light.'

Hearing this, my heart contracted.

'Have *you* ever seen the light?'

Regretfully, I shook my head.

'Sinners don't see it,' he said with conviction.

Nonplussed, I looked at the ground. I really was a sinner. My brother had told me this a number of times. Twice I had gone into the kitchen in the afternoon and eaten sugar, on the quiet. And I never told anybody, but, bawdy words such as my brother never uttered fell from my lips. That's why Mother had put red chillies into my mouth so many times. My face stayed pale like a sinner's while his face—and my brother's too—was red and kept glowing like the face of a celibate.

'You're standing here hiding and I've been searching for you for a whole hour.' It was Mother's strident voice coming from the staircase and echoing through the whole house.

All of us, boys and girls, ran to the staircase. In the middle of the staircase leading to the roof, Tulsi, standing with his back to the wall, was looking in Mother's direction.

'What are you doing standing here? Why didn't you answer when I called? Why don't you speak? Tell me what you were doing standing here.' At the foot of the staircase, all the boys and girls of the house stood looking upstairs in bewilderment. Mother was standing with her arms akimbo.

'Why don't you speak? What are these new tricks you are up to? You used to work perfectly well. Now what has gone wrong with you?'

Even now, Tulsi was still looking straight at Mother. I began to feel scared.

'What have you got hidden there? Tell me what it is. Have you started thieving now?'

Mother stepped forward, grasped his shirt, lifted it up, and pulled something out from his pyjama waist. It was a book.

'I gave it to him, Mamiji. He asked me for a book and I gave it to him,' said the girl with glasses, who was standing near me.

Mother, arms again akimbo, went on looking at him.

'For the last one hour, he's been sitting reading while I've been breaking my legs looking for him . . . What's the point in servants reading? If he was set on reading, why did he come here?'

Then, shaking her head, Mother said in an angry tone, 'If one's own family is unruly, what can anyone do? Now come down here. When on earth am I going to be finished with this work? It's already so late.'

Tulsi was still standing stockstill, like a statue. Never before had Mother gone on scolding Tulsi in such a loud voice in front of strangers.

'It's outrageous the way no work is done properly here. But then he'll only do the housework when he can take time off from his reading.'

Disheartened, Tulsi suddenly sat down. Putting his right arm on his knee, he made as if to hide his face in it, then his whole body started shaking. Seeing this, Mother promptly shouted, 'Look, look at what he's doing! Vidya, Vimla, why are you standing there gaping at me? Go and tell Father to come here.'

'Father isn't at home. He's gone out somewhere with Phoophaji.' I still couldn't understand what the matter was. Mother bent and shook Tulsi, but he didn't look up.

'Stop! Stop it!' she went on exclaiming as she shook him.

'See what a dreadful servant we've got! I didn't even say such a terrible thing to him that he should have bitten his own arm.'

Vidya came running upstairs and, along with Mother, started shaking Tulsi by the shoulder.

'Now what am I to do?' Mother's voice began to quaver.

'Where is he—Baldev's father? Baldev, what are you all standing there staring at?'

Tulsi removed his mouth from his arm and began sobbing convulsively. His deep, harsh voice sounded grotesque as he went on weeping.

Suddenly he got up and started off downstairs. Seeing so many people standing around, he went down the stairs like someone who had gone quite out of his mind, then, he went directly to the chhajja. On his right arm, bright red blood stains had formed into a ring.

'Vimla, go and fetch the pepper dish from the kitchen! Run!' And Mother too went towards the chhajja. We all wanted to go there, but our eldest sister from Kashmir stopped us.

That same night, my elder sister Vidya, standing beside the bed of the Kashmiri sister with glasses, was saying, 'Come on, let's go. Get up quickly!'

I heard this. My brother too heard this. The sister with glasses got up and started following close on Vidya's heels. My brother and I followed her very stealthily. It was dark in the courtyard but, up in the sky, there were a lot of stars shining brightly. Our own house seemed a strange place.

Both the sisters went into the bathroom and stood still there. We two brothers also reached there. Tulsi's voice could be heard coming from the chhajja. At first it was low, but then gradually became louder. Tulsi was saying his prayers before he went to sleep, just as Mother did, just as everyone in the house did, each sitting on his or her own bed:

'Oh God, give me the strength not to let the milk boil over, and let the cattle feed be ready on time.

'Oh God, it wasn't my fault that the chimney of the lamp broke in my hands. There was already a crack in it and, oh dear God, you surely know that I never sit idle. And may my sister Shanti remain well and happy. And my brother Amichand too . . .'

My sister Vidya couldn't control her laughter. So she was the first to run out of the bathroom. The rest of us, keeping close on her heels, ran back to the room.

I lay down back in my bed. I could hear Mother saying from the sitting room, 'At least things have improved. He used to pick quarrels wherever he went and would bite other people. Now he's only biting himself.'

And Mother started laughing. I could see one of mother's feet moving in the dark.

'He too will soon become an Arya Samajist,' said my Bua, and she too started laughing.

∽

Ages seem to have passed since then. The sounds of the neighbourhood haven't changed, but have somewhat lost their flavour. Things which formerly had loomed large, now seem to have shrunk and grown small. The four walls of the house have fallen down, as it were, and those casements, to which I used to remain glued watching our neighbourhood activities out in the street, are broken. I have stepped out of the house, and every single thing outside seems to draw me powerfully to itself like the eyes of a python. It seems a mere glimpse of the outside world has forced me to run out of the house. There is a flood of impressions . . .

Standing below the house with a chhajja which has blue, green and red windowpanes, stood a tonga. Two burqa-clad women got into it, and the tonga started coming towards our house. In front of Attar Singh's sweetmeat shop, I sprang on to the footboard. Feeling a weight fall on his footboard, the tonga driver swung his whip round to the back. I felt the sting of the lash on my back, and my whole body started burning. The whip also touched my right ear. But I still kept standing on the footboard. Before lashing out for the second time, the tonga driver turned around to have a look. 'My goodness, it's Babu's son!' He turned back again and looked straight ahead. The tonga was passing along new streets. On all sides, things seemed to be floating past my eyes—houses, roofs, clothes hanging out to dry, innumerable people on the streets. At every turning, the scene changed. Sometimes the houses were tall, sometimes low-built. Every day, I jumped on to the footboard of some tonga or the other and visited different parts of the town.

The monsoon rains were coming down in torrents. Clad in loincloths, my brother and I ran as far as Lunda Bazaar. The street gutters and the main open drain of the road were brimming over with brown muddy water.

I was sitting on the back of our horse Laloo, and my brother was walking alongside. We were going out of town to study in a *gurukul*. When the houses ended, vast fields came into view, extending as far as the mountains. Tulsi, be-turbaned and clad in Father's long coat, walked along, carrying our bags.

We reached the last house and Tulsi stopped. Catching hold of the horse's bridle, he helped me to dismount. Now it was my brother's turn. He would ride to the school and I would walk alongside. In the darkness of the innermost room of the gurukul, there was a very large creature. Tulsi said it was a peacock and that it was slowly dying. Sitting with the celibates, Tulsi ate chickpeas and jaggery and recited the rules of the *Ashtadhyayi*, Panini's famous treatise on grammar, consisting of eight chapters. At break time, he did push-ups with them.

Playing gulli-danda out in the street, we suddenly heard a noise. It was a woman's voice coming from the alley: 'Help! Save me! I'm being killed!'

We promptly ran towards the alley. The wall of Manohar's house was made of mud. A number of Muslim boys were already sitting on it. It was from the other side of this wall that a woman could be heard shrieking. I got on to a pile of bricks from which I could climb up on to the wall. A woman was lying on the ground. It was Manohar's new mother. His father was sitting on her chest and punching her. The woman's shirt was beginning to tear at the chest.

'I'm dying! Save me! I'm dying!' Close by on the ground, there was a small metal pot. Manohar's father moved forward and picked it up. Then he hit her really hard with it. She flung her head wildly from side to side. I couldn't see her face. A dark red fluid began to flow from her hair to the ground. The woman had stopped shrieking, but still went on tossing her head from side to side. Somebody began pounding on the alley door. 'Open the door, Bishen Dasji! Open the door!' It was my mother's voice. My Mother goes on rapping on the door . . .

Later on, Manohar explained to us that his new mother was a bad lot and that was why his father had beaten her.

The celibates, clad in saffron dhotis, were sitting in a row. My brother, also wearing a saffron dhoti, was sitting by Swamiji in the Arya Samaj. When Swamiji walked, the earth shook. When a real celibate walked, the ground trembled. My brother's thigh was becoming uncovered. The dhoti had fallen away from it. Swamiji picked up the end of the dhoti and covered his thigh. I hadn't been given a saffron dhoti to put on. I felt like bursting into tears.

In the Arya Samaj, the celibates lived upstairs. I crept up there stealthily and, finding a saffron dhoti in some celibate's cupboard, I took it out and put it on. I wrapped it around my legs again and again, but I didn't know how to tie it. Then I took it off and put it on again. Finally, standing right there, I burst out sobbing. From below, came the sounds of prayers being recited.

The day we had our sacred thread ceremony, I put on a saffron dhoti. The courtyard of the house was solidly packed with people. Before bathing, we had to sit so long in front of the barber with our heads bent that we started getting a backache. In one or two spots, our scalps got nicked by the razor. It caused a slight burning sensation, but I was happy. Very stealthily I went on running my hand over my clean-shaven head. Now my top-knot had thickened. My brother's head was also clean-shaven and he too now had a thick plait. Clad in our saffron dhotis and carrying white, three-cornered handkerchiefs knotted to form receptacles, we slowly made our way forward among the people sitting in the courtyard. Before each person I stopped and said, 'Please give alms!'

And they put in one or two annas, or some other coin, or even a currency note.

Moving forward, I said, 'Please give alms!'

I found it difficult to keep my dhoti from hanging askew.

Sitting by the sacred fire, our Panditji was gazing fixedly in our direction.

We then made our way through the crowd to return and we placed both the handkerchiefs in front of our guru. 'That is the fee paid to the spiritual preceptor,' said one Arya Samajist to another. 'Whatever the celibates bring, they first place at the guru's feet. It's an old custom. What a beautiful custom it is!'

But after the people had gone away, Mother and Father had a tiff. 'The guru went off with all the money. And you just sat there and watched him. You didn't even make a move to stop him.'

'The offerings are the guru's by right,' said Father mildly.

'What is this right he has, I'd like to know. The *acharya*s and pandits all take eight annas each. You've learnt new ways with these Arya Samajists. How do we know whether he has taken fifty or even a hundred with him? He stuffed the entire contents of the handkerchiefs into his pockets and walked off. People have lost all sense of shame. I'm going to take the money back from that so-and-so. I won't let him get away with it.'

Still clad in our saffron dhotis, we stood back against the wall feeling nervous. Father paced up and down with his hands behind his back.

'Now what can we do about it? Whatever he has taken is gone,' said Father quietly. At this, Mother spoke even more angrily. 'You were the one who let him get away. He walked off right before your eyes and left you gaping. That was when I was in the kitchen serving halwa to those good-for-nothings.'

'What are you going on about?' asked Father, stopping in the middle of the room. 'Aren't you grateful to God that the day has come when your sons have had their sacred thread ceremony? Did the pandit take the money out of your pocket? The money came from other people as an offering. On such a day, all one's utterances should be auspicious. May your sons remain safe and sound!'

Suddenly fearful, Mother fell silent and sat there like a statue. Slowly, Mother's expression turned into one of bewilderment. Why was Father talking of propitious and unpropitious things today? He had always expressed his disbelief in them. Was Father connecting such matters with our good health just to silence Mother?

The sound of footsteps on the staircase could be heard. Tulsi had caught hold of Panditji on the road outside and brought him in. Mother was still sitting, not saying a word. They crossed the courtyard, then both of them stopped in the doorway of the room. At that point, Mother joined her hands and, keeping them joined, said, 'Panditji, you went away without having a meal. You haven't had anything to eat or drink. You were going away without any kind of refreshments. It's quite unheard of.'

'I had some halwa, dear Mother.'

'No, no, you must have a meal before you go. Both of them are like sons to you. A guru is just like a father. Tulsi, spread a mat for Panditji, I'm just coming . . .'

§

'I'm not going to study in the gurukul,' said my brother.

'Why not?' asked Father, lifting his head from the typewriter and looking at him.

'I won't. I'll study in a regular school.' My brother said this, standing in the office, looking straight at Father. I had never seen him adopt this attitude before. He had stuck out his chin and was staring fixedly at Father. And he went on standing there quite calmly. I couldn't make any sense out of this at all. He had been given a saffron dhoti, but even so, he didn't want to study in the gurukul.

Father suddenly started laughing. When he laughs, his chin goes down into his neck. My brother just kept standing there.

'Don't study if you don't want to. I wanted you to study Hindi and Sanskrit, but I'll have you taught at home. You're just a little lad, but you're becoming quite daring.' And Father started laughing again, whereupon his chin disappeared into his neck. Then he got up from his chair and came over to us. Holding my brother under his right arm and me under his left, he kissed us on the head turn by turn.

'You are my right eye and he is my left eye.' So saying, he patted us on the back. 'If your heart's no longer in studying at the gurukul, don't study there. Study in a school . . .' And his eyes become moist.

ᵔ

Mother said to my sister, 'Vidya, go up on to the roof and bring four or five cow's dung cakes.'

'I'm not going, Mother. Send Tulsi.'

'You're not going, did you say?' Mother suddenly stops.

'Mother, I won't go upstairs . . .' And she whispers something into Mother's ear. She had just come down from the roof. I ran upstairs and looked through a peephole at the house across the road. The owner of the house was standing on the roof with his pyjamas off. He was stark naked. Whenever my sisters went up on to the roof, he would take his clothes off. I could hear Mother's footsteps on the stairs. The moment she came up, she started rebuking him. But as soon as he saw her, he went downstairs.

'The wretch! Father of five children! How wicked people can be!'

5

Father was pacing up and down the room with his hands behind his back and Mother, as always, was sitting on the bed. She was saying, 'Get her married this Baisakh. Don't delay it any longer.'

Father stopped in the middle of his pacing.

'What are you talking about? Do I have it in my power to perform it in Baisakh?'

'Now, my dear, why are you quarrelling with me? She's a grown-up girl. Pebbles are being tossed into the house every day. This neighbourhood is full of bad characters. Write to them to have the marriage ceremony performed this Baisakh.'

'The boy is studying. He will have his exams in Baisakh.'

'So let the marriage take place during the exams.'

'They say they want to have the wedding in the native village.'

'That's even better. I'll take the children to the village six months in advance. I'll make all the preparations there. Don't delay now. Send them a letter tomorrow.'

Father resumed his pacing.

'Why don't you forbid Vidya and Vimla to go up on to the chhajja?'

'Now look, my dear, how are these girls at fault? I neither let them go on to the chhajja, nor do I let them peep out of the windows. For years, I've kept them from their studies and made them sit at home, so that they wouldn't be seen in the streets. What more can I do? If ever they laugh out loud, even if it's only by accident, they still get a scolding. The whole day they sit in one room or the other.'

I kept listening and wondering if Mother would now tell about the roof—that when the sisters went up there, the rascal across the road would take off his clothes. But Mother didn't say anything. She concealed such things from Father, otherwise he would have promptly taken hold of his walking stick and gone out to pick a quarrel.

∽

A long time seemed to have passed. The uncertainties of childhood had to a great extent been sorted out. We brothers had stopped going to the gurukul and yes, Panditji was still coming to the house. When Baldev wrote, his handwriting was a work of art. The younger of my two elder sisters was much bigger than me, but even then, she fell ill very often. The elder sister, now married, no longer lived at home. At her wedding, I ate twenty paans, and in one place my feet got so stuck in the mud that one of my shoes got lost there and I came home crying. My brother-in-law had two of his teeth one behind the other, which struck me as being very beautiful. He said, 'When I was a child and my tooth broke, I kept rubbing my tongue on the space, so that my tooth grew in double.'

When my teeth broke, I kept rubbing my tongue in those places night and day, but I could never get them to grow in double.

For the wedding, we visited our native village. Boys were playing with marbles and there were donkeys wandering about, stirring up the dust. Then there was a lizard living below the staircase of the house. Mother said that if you tied a rope to its tail and threw it up, it would stick fast wherever its feet landed. Thieves and bandits used the lizard to help them climb over walls. The village used to have a high wall around it on all sides, but it is now all broken. And there were palaces inlaid with mirrors, but I never saw any of them. My mother's sister scolded the girls in a loud voice because they sang naughty songs at the wedding . . .

ॐ

It was the evening of a summer's day. The people of the house had finished their evening meal and were sitting and talking. As always, after everyone had finished eating, Mother was eating her food very slowly—two chapattis with vegetables on top of them, which she held in the palm of her hand. My brother was talking about some school matters. He had come first in his school and, in front of the whole class, the headmaster had kissed him and told him that he was going to send his name in for a scholarship examination.

A hurricane lamp on top of the tandoor cast a soft glow over the family members sitting in the courtyard. Sitting in the darkness with his back against the wall, Tulsi was scouring the utensils.

'Now they're going to make us boy scouts,' said my brother. 'We'll get khaki uniforms and all the scouts are to have a rope, a whistle and a staff!'

'Mother!' Tulsi's voice came out of the darkness.

My brother stopped speaking.

'What is it, Tulsi?' asked Mother, looking in the direction of the dark corner.

'Mother,' said Tulsi softly, 'am I going to spend my whole life scouring utensils?'

In a split second, everyone's attention turned to Tulsi. Everyone fell silent. Father, turning to look in his direction, said, 'If you don't clean utensils, what will you do? Don't all servants do such work? Have you suddenly become too delicate?'

Suddenly, gesturing in Tulsi's direction, Mother said, 'Stop now. That's enough. Stop right now. From now on you won't scour utensils.'

Tulsi stopped short, stupefied. In the middle of cleaning utensils in a basin, his hands came to a standstill. But he soon started cleaning them again.

Mother got up and took hold of his hand.

'Now I've told you, that's enough. From this moment onwards you won't clean utensils.'

It seemed to me that Mother was punishing Tulsi for having spoken out. She was dismissing him.

'Baldev's mother, what are you doing?' said Father. 'Let him clean the utensils. If he doesn't clean them, who will? Will you clean them?'

'Whether I clean them or somebody else cleans them, Tulsi won't clean them. This came from his heart. Now I won't have him clean utensils.'

So saying, Mother placed her hand on Tulsi's shoulder and tried to make him stand up. 'Now that's enough, son, you've been cleaning utensils in this house for sixteen years. That's long enough.'

Even then Tulsi went on looking at Mother's face in astonishment.

'What nonsensical things are you saying?' muttered Father. 'If he doesn't clean utensils, what will he do? Go on, Tulsi, get on with it, do your work.'

'I swear, on my life, that you will never touch another utensil. From today, your cleaning of utensils is at an end. Now get up from here and be off with you.'

We all gaped stupidly at Mother. Feeling further inspired, she said, 'He spoke out himself. I shall honour his words. Get up, son. What happens later will depend on your own good or bad fortune, but from now on I am not going to get you to clean utensils.'

'Have you taken leave of your senses?' muttered Father.

But Mother was becoming even more animated than before. She made Tulsi get up from where he had been sitting and, picking up the pan full of ash, she put it on top of the tandoor. Then she picked up a pot of water and poured water over Tulsi's hands. Bewildered, Tulsi looked at Father and Mother, turning his gaze from one to the other.

'Go and do whatever you please. You have never listened to anyone. Nor will you listen today,' said Father, and he got up from his mat and went towards the sitting room.

Sometime later, we all lay down on our beds. Silence had descended on the house, but we kept listening for sounds from the sitting room where, as usual, Father was walking up and down and Mother was sitting cross-legged on the bed.

'I have been telling you again and again that you should not have him study. What have servants to do with books? Now he finds housework irksome.'

Father went on pacing up and down the room with his hands behind his back. 'What harm is there in his studying for a bit? When he came to us, he was a completely uncouth creature. Education is man's greatest adornment.'

'So that is why he now feels scouring utensils to be humiliating. Why should I make him do it? Why should I have him do work which repels him? He was reared and grew up in this house along with my children. Before he started reading, this wasn't an issue. But now that he's literate, he doesn't like scouring utensils.'

Then silence fell between them. Only the sound of Father's footsteps could be heard. I judged from these sounds that Father had gone as far as the opposite wall, where Swamiji's picture was hanging, and that now he had turned back and come to the fireplace above which the clock was going tick-tock. Mother was sitting in the same place at the foot of the bed with both her hands in her lap.

Shortly afterwards, Mother's voice could be heard again: 'Keep him to do your office work. Set him to doing the clerical work.'

'There you go again! Do you imagine he could do office work? He doesn't know a single syllable of English. And my correspondence is either in English or in Urdu.'

Mother kept quiet for some time, then she said, 'If it wasn't going to be of any use to him, why did you continue to teach him only Hindi? He could have been taught Urdu too.'

'Why should I have had him taught Urdu? All our sacred scriptures are in Hindi.'

'But, my dear, what good are scriptures if they don't fill your stomach? . . . Keep him as a peon then and not as a clerk. He could go and meet your business associates and show them the samples.'

'That's enough. Let it be. Let him do the housework again from tomorrow. That's the only kind of work he can do.'

'No I won't get him to do any housework.'

'You are really very stubborn. If he doesn't do it, who will?'

'Look, my dear. Just try to understand. His hopes have been raised. Now, if he does housework, it will be with a very heavy heart. When your children go to study in schools and colleges, it will cause him mental anguish. Set him to some other sort of work. When you first put a school primer in his hands, I got tired telling you over and over again not to spoil his life. To let him be as he was. At that time, you didn't listen and you reduced me to silence with your scolding. Now that his hopes have been raised, he is no longer capable of doing housework . . .'

∽

I went downstairs to wash my hands and face. As usual, Tulsi was in the 'garage' preparing the cattle feed of chaff and oilcake mixed with water. Everything that had happened the night before came back to me. It seemed as if the previous day's conversation had all been in my imagination. Everything was going on as before. Tulsi was filling up the water vessels and sweeping the whole house. But when he started cleaning the utensils, I promptly called out to Mother. 'Look, Mother, Tulsi has started scouring the utensils again.' Mother came straight from the sitting room to the kitchen. Up till then, she had been sitting lost in thought.

'When you've already been told not to touch the utensils, why do you irritate me?'

'If I don't do it, who will?' asked Tulsi.

'How does it bother you? Anybody may do it.'

The family members congregated. Father had gone for a walk. Turning a deaf ear, Tulsi crouched with his head between his knees and started cleaning the utensils. Mother stood, arms akimbo, looking at him. Then stepping forward, she snatched the pan from him.

'I certainly won't allow you to do this. Get up now, do you hear?' Tulsi came forward and clasped Mother's feet.

'Mother, I made a mistake. It just slipped out. I didn't mean anything by it. Please forgive me . . .'

'Just see now what a stubborn person he is! He doesn't even listen to anybody.'

Tulsi got up and went and sat for a long time on the upper staircase in a state of dejection.

A few days perhaps after this, I went upstairs for a drink of water. As usual, arriving outside the kitchen, I called out to Tulsi for water. But nobody answered me. I called out again and peeped into the kitchen. No sign of Tulsi. I went on to the chhajja where Tulsi's torn durrie was always spread out. Tulsi wasn't there, and nor was his durrie. I ran to the balustrade. Downstairs, the entire household was standing outside Father's office. Tulsi, wearing a turban and coat was standing in the middle of them. I ran downstairs. In the rear, a small bundle had been put by the wall on the ground. In the corner was a staff which Tulsi had brought, perhaps years ago, from his village.

'Tulsi is leaving,' said my brother in an undertone.

'Come here, Tulsi!' It was Father calling from inside.

Tulsi was standing stock still, as always.

'Come along, take this letter.'

Stepping forward, Tulsi fell at Father's feet. His turban came undone and one end of it hung down on his neck.

Letting go of Father's feet, he clasped Mother's feet with both hands and put his head on them.

'Come on, get up now. This letter is to be given to Vaidji. Say that I have talked to Lala Sant Ram.'

Tulsi was very slow to get up and this annoyed Father. 'Now will you get up! Are you going to let me do any work or not?'

My brother told me Tulsi had got a job. 'Now he will work in the dispensary run by the Arya Samaj gurukul.'

Just as he stood up, Father said, 'All right, wait a bit. Go in an hour's time. You can post two or three of my letters on the way.'

At this, Mother said disapprovingly, 'Now look, my dear, what are you doing? You have big sons. Can't they post the letters? Will you have the letters posted by him today too?'

'What have I said, my dear lady? Is he going to a foreign country? What will happen if he sets off one hour later? If he posts two of my letters on the way, will the henna come off his hands? Here, Tulsi, take this letter and go. Put your back into the work there, don't sleep over it the way you did here. The harder you work, the greater will be your success.'

Mother took me aside and said into my ear, 'There's a bowl of oil on the kitchen fireplace. Run and fetch it.' As I turned, Mother cautioned me, 'Don't say anything to Father. Not so much as a whisper. Bring it down to the courtyard. I'm coming there.'

When I brought down the bowl of oil, Mother was already standing in the courtyard. Vimla too was there, looking very pale. Her eyes were wet.

As Mother took the bowl from my hand, she said, 'Let's hope your Father doesn't come here.' Then she poured a little oil on either side of the threshold. But Tulsi wasn't coming towards the courtyard. His voice too was no longer audible. My brother entered the courtyard. He said, 'Actually, Mother, Tulsi has left. He went out through the office door.'

Mother bit her lip. She became extremely despondent. I immediately took a look outside. Tulsi had reached the manger. He had his staff on his right shoulder and was carrying his bundle in his left hand. With his coat and his turban, he seemed like a stranger.

'Well, may God keep him safe and sound! Wherever he may go, let him be happy!' said Mother softly. Then, once again, she sprinkled drops of oil at either end of the doorstep. Then giving the bowl back to me, she went off in the direction of the office. When I returned after putting the bowl back in the kitchen, all the family members were sitting in Father's office. When Father wasn't typing out letters, he would sit with his head tilted to one side, looking out of the window. Mother was sitting on the leather bench, both her legs dangling. Vimla was sitting beside her and my brother was standing next to the fireplace.

After a little while, Father said very softly, 'To be sure, the gurukul people have taken on my man on my say-so, but you can count upon them to rub it into me hundreds of times.'

'You supported him. That's a very great thing. Now whatever happens to him will be a matter of his own luck!'

Father again looked out of the window and after a short time, he said, shaking his head, 'Tulsi is very simple at heart. He's guileless. And honest, too.'

Mother remained silent. Father, still looking outside, went on saying, 'But he was thick-headed. He's a dimwitted person.' He shook his head at this assertion, then again said, 'He's a dimwit. He will never amount to anything. He's too block-headed.'

'Look, my dear, he has only just left the house. You should be wishing him luck. You should only be thinking of the good of someone who has gone away.'

'What have I said? He will achieve something only if he exerts himself. Success is not to be had just by reciting scriptural verses.'

Mother wanted to say something, but she kept quiet.

∽

My brother had taken the quilt off his face. He wasn't in the habit of sleeping with his head under the quilt. But I liked to sleep right under the quilt with my knees drawn up to my chest and both my hands between my thighs.

'Turn and face me,' I said to him.

'No. Go to sleep. I'm feeling sleepy.'

'You pushed me over to the edge of the bed and you've pulled the quilt away too. My back is getting uncovered.'

'Don't talk. Vimla is ill. Go to sleep.'

'Father hasn't come. Won't Father sleep here?'

'Father is in her room. Go to sleep.'

A few days before, they had brought her back from Lahore. When they brought her into the house, she was laid down on the wheeled cot. There was a white sheet spread on it, with which she was also wrapped up. Only her nose and cheeks were visible. Father didn't let us go near her.

For a long time that day, Father stood talking to Dr Ram Narayan in a corner of the sitting room. He was taller even than Father. If I had gone to them, Father would have sent me away. He was mentioning an English doctor by the name of Harrison and saying that Vimla's face was swollen.

I said to myself, over and over again, that my sister was ill and that her face was swollen, but this didn't have any effect on me. Everyone in the house was silent. But for me to keep quiet became impossible.

'Come on, let's go outside. That man is sure to have come. Let's see.'

'Who?' asked my brother, turning over.

'The one who comes every evening. You said to point him out to you when he came.'

'First of all, go and see.'

I got out of bed and, instead of going on to the chhajja, I quietly crossed the terrace and went downstairs. Right in the middle of the staircase, there was a very small window which opened on to the street. I took a quick look outside. That man was indeed standing in front of the house. He had his hands behind his back and was looking up at the chhajja. Who was this man? Why was he coming here? Why didn't he knock at the door and come in? I watched him in silence for a while, then quickly went back upstairs into the room.

'He's really standing outside. Come and see.' I shook my brother by the shoulder. 'He has come again today.'

In the meantime, my brother had dozed off. Turning over to face me, he said, 'Who has come? And don't address me as "you". Call me "brother".'

'The one who comes every day. He's standing down below, dear brother!'

It seemed to me in the darkness that my brother was studying my face. Then he suddenly got up, crossed the room and went out barefooted. I followed right behind him. The two of us peeped out of the small window on the staircase. In the darkness, the man seemed to waver like a shadow. My brother kept looking at him for a long time.

'Now he has started coming every day. He came yesterday too.'

'He is about to become our brother-in-law. Our sister Vimla is going to get married to him. His name is Jaswant,' said my brother.

'How do you know?'

'I know,' said my brother, and went off upstairs and straight into the old sitting room to Mother.

In a corner by the fireplace, four women were sitting in silence. A soft glow fell on them from the hurricane lamp above it. All four of them sat in the same way. No one said a word. All of them had their dupattas over their heads. The fourth woman was our Maasi. When had she arrived? How small she looked sitting next to our Bua! At the back was a green wooden cupboard on which lines had been drawn in chalk. Between them was written, 'This cupboard belongs to Vimla.' Our sister Vidya was sitting at the foot of the cupboard. At that time, she too was at home and was using the room next to the kitchen. Her stomach had become very big.

'Mother, Jaswant is standing down below in the street. Every evening he comes and after a while, he goes away.'

Mother slowly lifted her head. The soft glow of the lamp fell on her features. Her eyes had a drawn look about them. She had never looked like that before.

'Mother, Jaswant has come and he's downstairs,' repeated my brother.

Mother looked at him out of creased, screwed-up eyes. She nodded slowly to let him know that she had heard him.

My brother went back without a word and we both lay down again on the bed. The house was quiet as before.

Father was still in my sister's room. The clock on the wall chimed eleven. I gradually dozed off. Suddenly, I woke up with a start. It was Father's voice. 'Recite mantras,' he was saying. 'Our dear Vimla wants us to recite mantras.' His voice was quavering.

Then he himself began saying mantras in a faltering voice.

Maasi joined in, followed first by Bua, then by our sister Vidya, sitting at the foot of Vimla's cupboard.

Only Mother was not reciting mantras.

Should we too recite mantras? I knew them by heart, but I couldn't speak. My brother was lying quietly with his back to me. At times, Father's footsteps could be heard. Was he pacing up and down at this time too? Why had these people started reciting mantras now? Why did Vimla want us to recite mantras? My sister Vimla was ill, her face was swollen—I repeated these words to myself, but they had no effect on me. They all went on reciting mantras for a very long time.

'She's gone! Vimla has gone!' Father's trembling voice could be heard in the middle of the prayers.

'Vidya, my dearest one, your sister has gone.'

'*Haayee*!' came Maasi's voice. 'Haayee, Vimla, my child!'

Everyone began weeping and lamenting.

My brother immediately got out from under the bedclothes. Even then I had no clear understanding of what had happened. It was dark in the room. A feeble glow was coming into the room from the old, dimly lit sitting room.

My brother got down from the bed and went straight into the old sitting room. Following on his heels, I too went there. Father was standing in the middle of the room. He had on all his day clothes, even his turban and his coat. The crest of Father's turban, which was always tucked into it, was hanging down. He held it up and wiped his eyes with it and sometimes stuffed it into his mouth. My elder sister, looking weary, was sitting on the floor with her back to the wall and her knees drawn up. Her head was tilted to one side and her face was half-hidden beneath her hair.

My brother immediately went into the room. He never asked anybody before he did anything, he would just go ahead and do it. I didn't want to go into the room.

My elder sister wept and writhed, and a muffled shriek issued from her lips. All the women—and I too—immediately turned around and looked at her. What was happening to Mother's face? Her eyes were screwed up and squinting and her lips seemed to have withered away.

My brother came out of the room and went on looking at the lamp, his eyes dilated. Then, picking up the lamp, he took it into the room where our sister Vimla was lying. I didn't want to go into the room. After a short time, my brother came back with the lamp in his hand and put it above the fireplace. Standing in front of it, he went on looking blankly in front of him. How wide open his eyes were, wide open and with a fixed stare! How creased up Mother's eyes were becoming!

Every now and again, one or another of the three women would start to lament.

'I am not worthy of your trust, oh Lord, I couldn't keep your trust,' said Father. 'Go along, children, go, go to sleep.'

The clock chimed two.

My elder sister sobbed, then cried out, clenched her fists and bit her lips. All three women turned round to her again. Maasi and Bua were looking at Mother.

'Get up, Vidya, my dear,' said Maasi. 'Get up and let's go to your room.'

Both Maasi and Bua got up, and holding on to my sister's arms, helped her up. Then, giving her support, they very slowly took her out through the door. Mother got up. What had happened to my sister Vidya?

'Please sit down, my dear sister,' said Maasi. But Mother stepped forward. 'No.' And so saying, she left the room.

'Go, Baldev, go children, go, go to your room.'

We went back to bed again. Silence fell upon the house once more. Now even Father's pacing couldn't be heard. But someone was moving about in the courtyard. Maasi's footsteps could be heard—she dragged her feet when she walked. She was going downstairs. Where was Maasi going?

Suddenly, cleaving the darkness came the sound of my sister Vidya shrieking. Why had they taken her to her room? Why was she shrieking so loudly?

Was my sister Vidya too dying?

'Oh Lord! Only you can give us support.' It was Father's voice. 'Have mercy on us, Oh Lord, have mercy on us!'

Father started pacing up and down again.

'What a night this is! Oh God, have mercy on us, oh Lord, have mercy on us!'

It seemed as if Father were standing in the street and speaking in a very loud voice.

My sister was screaming again. This was the longest time she had gone on screaming. There was a sound of footsteps in the courtyard. Was it Bua? Or Mother?

Downstairs, the outside door was opened and there were sounds of footsteps on the stairs. Very rapid footsteps. Had Maasi come back? Who had come with her?

Suddenly, the heavy silence and darkness were riven by the crying of a child, 'Ah—eh—ah—eh!'

'Praise be to God. Only you can succour us, oh Lord!' said Father in the next room.

We two brothers got up and came to the door. Maasi's tiny frame was visible in the doorway of the sitting room. She said, softly, 'May the Lord be praised. Vidya has a daughter.'

At this, Father said in a quavering voice, 'Vimla has come back to us. God has sent her back to us.' And he began to weep.

The crying of a tiny baby was heard again.

In the soft, flickering light of the hurricane lamp, Father's shadow at times assumed frightening proportions. 'Write *Om* on the child's tongue! Write it with honey,' said Father. 'Baldev, go and tell your mother to write Om on the baby's tongue.'

Outside in the courtyard, it was pitch-dark. The walls of the house were very high and looked frightening. In the open expanse of the sky, countless stars were shining. I looked at them and thought I was dreaming.

The door of my sister's room was closed. We peeped in through the cracks. In the dim light I could see a very small part of the bed. The sound of a baby crying seemed to be coming from that direction.

'Father said to write Om on the baby's tongue with honey.'

Mother opened one side of the door just a little. She didn't let us slip inside. 'So it's you,' she said softly and, putting out her hand, she began to stroke my brother's head. Her movements seemed trance-like.

Then she closed the door and we two went back to bed.

After a little while, very quiet sobbing could be heard again from the old sitting room.

॰

The door of the dispensary was closed. The big gate of the Arya Samaj too was shut. Above the closed door of the dispensary was written in very large letters: 'Charitable Dispensary.' It was here that Tulsi worked. The sun's first rays were just touching the walls of the houses. They hadn't yet reached the street. With a small bundle tucked under my arm, I peeped in through the closed gate of the dispensary. The large courtyard was empty. To the right, the platform in the prayer room too was empty. On the opposite wall, above each arch of the veranda, very short sayings from the Vedas were inscribed in different colours:

Speak the truth.
Follow the path of righteousness.
Self-realization never comes to the timid.
Hard is that path, say the poets.
Speak the truth, speak pleasantly.

Downstairs, the courtyard was empty. Tulsi was nowhere to be seen. I moved away and went round to the side of the dispensary from which a broad street led downwards. Two boys were examining a dead snake, turning it over and over with a stick. The head of this catechu-coloured snake had been crushed. The boys left the snake alone and, after a short time, it began to move. It started to crawl ever so slightly. A little way off, there was a rubbish heap with a large trash can beside it.

Suddenly I saw Tulsi emerging from behind the trash can. He was carrying two buckets spilling over with water. And he was about to cross the street. He was bareheaded and just as robust and stocky as before. When he saw me, his face lit up.

'It's been a long time since you last came,' he said in his gruff voice, laughing and showing his bright red gums.

'I came to give you something,' I said, putting the bundle in front of him. 'Mother has sent some clothes.'

I had hardly finished speaking when there was a shout from somewhere: 'Now why on earth have you stopped there? Just see how late it's getting.' Across the street, about twenty steps up, a woman was standing on the landing of a house and shouting at Tulsi. One leg of her salwar was pulled up to the knee. With a broom in her hand and a twig for cleaning teeth lodged in her mouth, she was waiting for Tulsi.

Tulsi said to me, 'Just wait for a bit. I'll be back after washing the staircase of Vaidji's house. You go on up to my room.'

And he picked up the buckets and crossed the street. I stood there for some time watching Tulsi. I had come with very different expectations. I had thought there would be a crowd of patients at the dispensary and Tulsi, clad in his coat and turban, would be busy making up and handing out packages of medicines. But here he was—washing stairs. Was he doing housework here too? My brother had been saying Tulsi would become a doctor.

There were about twenty very high steps. Tulsi, with his buckets spilling over, had reached the landing. The woman, who had tangled hair, had pulled up the other leg of her salwar a little bit. Tulsi poured the water and she started sweeping the steps. Tiny rivulets of muddy water started flowing down. Having poured out two buckets of water, Tulsi returned with the buckets and the woman, her salwar legs now hitched up to the knee, stood working her jaws as she chewed the twig in her mouth. 'Hurry up!' she shouted. 'Don't die down there.'

I went in from the rear and slowly climbed the stairs up to the third floor where Tulsi Ram's room was.

As I stepped inside, a shadowy figure moved away from the window, crossed the room and huddled in one corner. A yellow dupatta floated in front of me and there was a clink of glass bangles. This was Devaki, Tulsi Ram's wife. Some time ago, after their wedding, Tulsi had brought her from the village.

I stood hesitantly on the doorstep. Devaki was standing with her back to me and facing the corner.

'Mother has sent these clothes,' I said softly. At this, she turned round, but bashfully stayed where she was. I put the bundle on the floor. I had seen Devaki once before, when Tulsi had brought her along after their wedding in the village and Mother, on that occasion, had given her some clothes.

Even now, Devaki was wearing my sister Vidya's clothes.

'He's downstairs. Please sit down,' she said, gesturing towards a cane mat spread out on one side next to the wall.

A number of shining utensils had been placed right in front of it. On the other side of the room, there was a mud fireplace. On the other side of the cane mat against the wall, on the floor, there were a few books. This was Tulsi's own house.

'He has gone to wash the staircase, he'll be coming.'

For some time she stood hesitantly in the corner, then she dashed out of the right-hand door opening on to the roof, and stood looking out of the small window set beneath the parapet. I understood. From this window, the house of the *vaidya*, the traditional physician, could be seen, and Devaki had her gaze fixed on Tulsi. I also got up from the cane mat and went to the window and started looking down in the same direction.

Having poured out the water, Tulsi, was carrying both the empty buckets downstairs. Reaching the last step, he turned his gaze upwards and smiled. His eyes were perhaps seeking Devaki through the window.

It had taken two buckets of water to clean one staircase. But it was so clean that it shone. Some of the bricks stood out bright red.

Tulsi's face was glowing. Every now and then, as he was going down, he looked up and smiled. This smile wasn't for me, it was for Devaki, who stayed glued to the window, watching him.

The vaidya must be getting the staircase washed every day because he liked cleanliness. Now Tulsi had reached the very middle of the staircase and was pouring the water and also doing the sweeping himself. The physician's wife still stood on the landing, working her jaws and hurling abuse at him.

Tulsi started sweating. The back of his kurta deepened in colour. The sun was starting to become fierce.

It was a very long time before Tulsi came back to the room. As soon as he had finished washing the staircase, he went into the vaidya's house to pour water there too.

'Deviji, give me a little water,' said Tulsi, wiping the sweat from his forehead with his sleeve. He called his wife 'Deviji', addressing her as a benevolent goddess, as was customary in certain Arya Samaj households.

'The secretary's man had come,' said Devaki in a complaining tone as she handed Tulsi a glass of water. 'The secretary wants you to have the brazier for the ritual fire brought to his house from the chairman's house.'

'When did he come?'

'He came just a little while ago.'

Standing in the middle of the room, Tulsi began to look very small. Now he didn't look very big to me.

'You had to carry twenty-four buckets today,' she said with a touch of pain in her voice.

Laughing, Tulsi turned towards me. 'I fill up all the buckets one after another and carry them up, while she stands upstairs and keeps counting them.'

'Yesterday, there were twenty-eight, and the day before that, twenty-nine,' said Devaki, her voice beginning to falter. 'I sit idle here at home when I could be washing the stairs. But he doesn't let me do it,' she said, her throat constricted. Then she hid her head between her knees.

'But do I ever get tired? I can carry fifty buckets.' Addressing me, Tulsi said, 'The vaidya's wife is very keen on cleanliness. I have to fill up twenty to twenty-five buckets of water every day. I don't get time to read.'

Tulsi had taught Devaki the verses of the prayer—morning, noon and evening prayers as well as the *Shanti Path* hymn—and was teaching her to read from the primer.

I pushed the small bundle sent by Mother towards Devaki.

'Mother has sent some clothes,' I said once again.

Devaki's eyes began to sparkle. She promptly came forward, opened up the bundle and started looking at the clothes. They were old clothes which had belonged perhaps to Vimla, or to Vidya. There were also some baby clothes among them, and when Devaki opened them up she became red with embarrassment. Then she hid her face in them with a clinking of bangles.

'Now I'll be off. I have to deliver the brazier for the havan. Then the dispensary opens at 8.30. I'll be late.' Tulsi's eyelids began to droop. It looked as if he were about to drop off to sleep sitting there on the cane mat with his back against the wall.

'Oh, good heavens!' said Devaki suddenly and, getting up, she went to the cooking fire.

'What are you going to do, Deviji?'

'I'll quickly cook you two chapattis. Eat something before you go.'

'Where is the time to eat anything now? Is this any time to be eating? The chairman's house is in a new locality. I have to get the brazier for the havan from there and take it to the Saidpuri Mohalla. And it will also be opening time for the dispensary here.'

When Tulsi was with us in our home, he was the servant of a family. But here he was the servant of scores of Arya Samaj members.

'Please have just one chapatti, my dear. How late you get coming home!' Then, looking at me, she said, 'Every day he eats at odd times. Sometimes he's out the whole day on an empty stomach. Somebody or the other keeps calling him away. Please ask Father to speak to the doctor.'

'I'm not having anything to eat.' There was something of Father's tone in Tulsi's voice. He got up from the cane mat, yawned and stretched his limbs, then went to the window. 'Vaidji is coming,' he said. Devaki also leapt to the peephole and looked out. I too came to the window. It was indeed the physician. He had come out of his house and was slowly descending the staircase. He had on a turban and spectacles and a coat which came down to below his knees.

'Look, my dear,' twittered Devaki, 'Vaidji is going to come half-way down and then go back up again, you can count on his going back once at least.'

And that's exactly what happened. The vaidya came down about a dozen steps, hesitated, and then went back up again.

Devaki giggled loudly, like a little girl. 'Now you know what?' she warbled. 'Vaidji has gone to get his bag.' And again she stood right against the window looking out. This guess of hers also turned out to be correct. The physician returned and he really had a large lentil-green bag in his hand—the kind which is tied on horses' mouths. This time, Devaki clapped her hands and laughed.

'You shouldn't laugh at your elders, Deviji. I've explained this to you several times,' said Tulsi in his deep, gruff voice. Tulsi's tone of voice was really beginning to resemble my father's.

The doctor's wife too had come out on to the landing and was standing there saying something to him. Devaki came away from the window at that point, looking rather downcast. 'They're going to send you to the market today for groceries. Just you wait and see. Please go downstairs now quickly, otherwise Vaidji will come and call out for you.'

'What are you saying, Deviji? You mean I shouldn't fetch Vaidji's groceries? Such words shouldn't even come to your lips,' said Tulsi in a scolding tone.

We started going down the stairs, Devaki stood glumly in the doorway.

'Tulsi, are you going to become a doctor?' I asked as we were going down the lower staircase.

'Vaidji only teaches me in fits and starts. I don't actually get the time.' Then, as if talking to himself, he said, 'I'm going to take Devaki back to the village. I'll cook two chapattis for myself. Then perhaps I'll be able to study.'

At the foot of the stairs, the vaidya was standing with his bag. With his hands folded, Tulsi approached him.

'Here, Tulsi Ram, take this bag and bring a few things from the shops,' said the vaidya, and handed him a list.

§

It was afternoon. Outside the kitchen, my brother and I were talking under the tin roof. My brother, wearing a khaki solar hat was leaning against a column. He had come from Lahore for the holidays. He was wearing white trousers. I went on looking at his hat. 'We wear it tilted to one side, like this,' he said, tipping it slightly over his right temple. He looked very fair. His face was glowing.

'These are our college colours,' he said, displaying a necktie which he took out of his suitcase. It had gold and red stripes. 'The boys also wear a blazer in these colours.'

'What is a blazer?'

'It's a jacket made of special cloth. I haven't brought it with me.'

Exactly as before, a new world started opening up before my eyes as I listened to my brother talk.

'Our sports shirts too are in these colours. So are our towels and jerseys and stockings,' said my brother. 'We are taught by English professors there. Two of our professors are English.'

Just to keep my end up, I immediately came out with, 'I've started shaving.' Only two days earlier, I had shaved for the first time. My cheeks had got cut by the new blade and I bled here and there.

'Why have you started shaving so soon?' asked my brother seriously, sitting down on the bed beside me.

'Jet black hairs were growing on my chin. If I had plucked them out, even thicker hairs would have appeared.'

'Whom did you ask before you started shaving? In the very beginning, the hairs are actually cut with scissors. Now your beard will be hard to shave. Just wait and see. Your face will be all beard.'

I kept gazing despondently at his face. Nothing I did ever pleased my brother. Whatever little enthusiasm I had worked up now gave way to despair.

'Just see how soft the shaven part of my face is,' he said and took my hand and passed it over his cheeks. His cheeks were really very soft, whereas mine were becoming roughened. I again felt inferior to my brother.

'At night I also have wet dreams,' I said in a soft, hurt voice.

My brother looked at me for a bit. I had never thought anyone's eyes could grow so large.

'How often has this happened?'

'Three times. The first time was in summer. I told Mother. It was as if some pus had come out of me. I got very frightened.'

'What did Mother say?'

'Mother didn't say anything, but she told Father.'

'Then? What did Father say?'

'Father gave me a severe scolding,' I said, lowering my voice. 'He said, "You must have been reading novels," and picked up one of my prescribed books and threw it out of the window. Now he gets me up at four o'clock every morning and tells me to bathe in cold water.'

'So?'

'He gave me a book to read. In it was written that that was semen.'

'I too have read that. *Drops of Nectar*—isn't that what it's called?'

'Yes! It also said you should always chew your food before swallowing it and that you should bathe every evening in cold water.'

'How many times do you chew your food?'

'Seventy times. I swallow only when the food in my mouth has turned to water. And every day in the morning and evening, I bathe with cold water.'

'Do you drink milk? You shouldn't drink milk at night.'

'No. Even if Mother gives it to me, I don't drink it. I used to eat four chapattis at night but now I eat only one.'

'Do you exercise?'

'Yes, I run along with a friend of mine as far as Chakalala and we also run all the way back.'

'Then,' said my brother, averting his eyes from me and speaking as if he were a doctor, 'you shouldn't be having nocturnal emissions. Who is this friend of yours?'

'You know him, Kuldip, Dharmdev's younger brother.'

'Does he too have wet dreams?'

'I don't know. I don't talk to anybody about it.'

My voice had become even lower than before. Then I mentioned the book again. '. . . and it says you shouldn't look at women.'

'Do you do that?'

'Sometimes I do, but not on purpose,' I said quite frankly. 'When some woman takes off her burqa in the alley, I can't help but see her,' I added in guilt-ridden tones. 'One day, I was standing on the roof. I called downstairs to Mother, and Akaran, in the house behind ours, mimicked me, shouting, "Mother." I looked, and it was Murtaza's sister. She's grown very big. She was looking right at me and laughing.'

My brother started looking at me again.

'But I promptly went downstairs.' My brother still remained silent.

'I tore up all the pictures of women out of my books.'

'How many days elapse between your wet dreams?'

'The second time was after twenty-seven days and the third was after twenty-six days.'

'How do you know? Do you keep counting the days?'

'Yes, I count each day.'

'Do you masturbate?' My brother suddenly asked me. He was looking at me fixedly.

'Of course not, I don't even touch my body.'

'Do you swear by Father that you don't masturbate?'

'I don't do it, I swear by Father.'

My brother didn't believe me.

'Put your hand on my heart and say that you don't masturbate.'

I put my hand on my brother's heart and said, 'I don't do it.'

'Say that you don't masturbate.'

'I don't masturbate.'

'Now take Surender. You know Surender, don't you?'

'Yes.'

'He used to masturbate. His organ turned blue.'

I kept looking at my brother.

'The doctor put tincture of iodine on his organ. Now when he starts to masturbate, his organ pains.'

After a short pause, my brother said, 'People who masturbate get dark shadows under their eyes and they grind their teeth. Do you grind your teeth?'

'Of course not.' Then I quietly asked my brother, 'Do you get wet dreams?'

'No! Just once or twice every five or six months. But when it's about to happen, I take very deep breaths and it stops. Then I immediately jump out of bed and do push-ups and deep knee bends. Then it doesn't happen.'

My brother's complexion looked healthy, like that of a true celibate. His eyes shone and his cheeks were pink and white. I thought I had already fallen by the wayside and that was why my complexion was dull and sallow, with no freshness about it.

'Tell me, what should I do?' I asked in bewilderment.

My brother sat opposite me, thinking. His attitude was still that of a doctor. I was so worried about getting my brother to believe me on this point that I said very quietly, 'I've also given up sleeping at night.'

'What do you mean?' He looked at me in surprise.

'If you don't go to sleep, you can't have a wet dream. When everyone in the house has gone to sleep, I get out of bed and go downstairs into Father's office, and keep sitting in front of the clock on the wall.'

'You keep sitting the whole night?'

'Yes, till four o'clock. I do feel very sleepy, but to stop myself from falling asleep, I sometimes count the seconds by the clock, and sometimes I just keep counting. At other times, I pace up and down.'

'Do you do this every day?'

'No, I don't do this for a few days after I've had a wet dream, but after about ten days or so, I start feeling afraid that someday I might have another wet dream. Then I don't sleep.'

My brother was still looking at me.

'I've also stopped cycling,' I said. 'In the book it's written that if you go cycling you get more wet dreams.' Then I quietly added, 'Now I also tie on a G-string.'

My brother didn't say a word.

'Tell me, what am I to do?' I said, looking at my brother in great confusion.

He thought for a moment, then said quietly, 'I'll ask my professor. We'll do whatever he says. During these holidays I'll put a stop to your wet dreams.'

The beds had been laid out in the courtyard and all the family members were happily asleep. There was a gentle breeze and countless stars were twinkling in the sky. They seemed washed clean in their radiance. I lay, holding my breath, on the bed, till Father dropped off to sleep. The sound of bangles jingling came from next door. After a little while, some man got up to drink water. It was a good thing there was some noise, otherwise I might have dozed off. I raised myself a little on my elbows. If you keep lying in bed on your back, you never know when sleep might overtake you. But if you keep moving, turning from side to side, raising your head, or just sitting for a minute, you can keep sleep at bay. If there is a sound of a footstep, that helps slightly to keep you alert.

Father let out a snore. I immediately got up. In the next bed my brother was in deep sleep. My heart began to throb wildly. How I wished I too could fall into a deep sleep! My brother never ever got up in a state of agitation the way I did, time and time again. In the morning the sun would come up, but he would go on sleeping.

I tiptoed to Father's office, took the chain off the door and went in. As I went in, the clock chimed the half-hour. But there was only one chime. Was it half past one or one o'clock? The room was pitch-dark. I became conscious of my breathing. If I put on the electric light for a second, I'd be able to see the right time on the clock. But no, if Father saw a light in his office he would get up and ask all sorts of questions.

I could hear the regular tick-tock of the pendulum. I started walking to and fro in the office. It was twelve paces from Father's table to the rear wall. Sometimes it was eleven and a half. On one occasion, I had walked a total of 600 steps, until I saw the rays of the early morning sun through the skylight which opened on to the street. Now, I should keep walking at least until the clock chimed, so that I could find out the correct time. The time between two-thirty and four was dangerous. If I failed to remain alert and if I lay down, I ran the risk of having a wet dream. I felt stifled in the heat, walking up and down inside the room with all the doors closed. My shirt, wet with perspiration, clung uncomfortably to my back.

Should I sit down for a little while on the couch? I made a silent vow that I would sit up straight, that I would not lean against the back of the couch and that I would count up to fifty and then stand up. I just wanted to sit down for a little while. But my feeling of dread wouldn't let me. No. I would walk another two hundred paces before sitting down. As I walked in the darkness, some parts of the office seemed blacker than others. It seemed that the office was divided into different shades of darkness.

I had done only 150 paces when my back started hurting. At times I would stagger a little to the right or left. Then I would stand still with my hand on a chair, and I would blink hard. This also helped to keep sleep at bay.

The clock chimed twice. I had expected that on the second occasion it would chime only once, which would mean that it was one-thirty. But now another half-hour had elapsed, which was like a bonus. Now I could sit down for a short time.

But no. I wouldn't sit on the couch. The couch was well-stuffed and soft. I would sit on the floor and lean my head against it. In this position, even if I dozed off, there would be no fear of having a wet dream because, then, I wouldn't be lying down at all. I'd be sitting. The couch was really very soft. Should I sit on it for just a minute? Sweat had started running down my back again. My head kept lolling on to the couch and I couldn't lift it. I couldn't keep it upright. It seemed to me that I was sinking, sinking into peaceful depths . . . I woke with a start. I had had a dream. What was this dream? I was lying on my bed and it was a moonlit night. In a vast and beautiful ravine, the silvery light shone far and wide, right up to the foot of some mountain. My pillow was soft, extremely soft! And so, because of its softness, my whole body was drenched in this moonlight which shone in every direction. I immediately got up and took very deep breaths . . .

I had saved myself from having a wet dream. I kept on taking deep breaths. Then I stood up and started walking. Now that I had slept for a little while, I wouldn't fall asleep again. Disaster had been imminent, but I had been saved. I had escaped by a hairbreadth. If I had had a wet dream, I would at that time have been breaking my head against the wall or I would have been thinking of running away from home.

Should I just for once put on the light and see the time? If I hadn't dozed off, I would have had an idea of the time. Not knowing the time made me feel I had plunged into deep waters. My neck was a little sore, which meant I had had a long nap. 'Oh God! Oh Lord Satchidanand!' It was Father's voice. He would be getting up now. He regularly got up once after two-thirty. I was afraid that his gaze would fall on my empty bed. I stood in the middle of the office, holding my breath. Having got up, Father moved ponderously in the direction of the bathroom. I kept listening for sounds from the terrace. If Father saw the empty bed and called out, what would happen? I would sneak out of the office, go into the courtyard and say that I had been up on the roof. But Father had come back and was drinking water that he had poured from a narrow-necked earthenware vessel. 'Oh God! Oh Lord Satchidanand!' He repeated this once again, then lay down on his bed. He didn't look in the direction of my bed.

I again started pacing up and down and counting the number of steps. If there had been light in the room, there would have been fewer chances of my falling asleep. Then I could have sat and fixed my gaze on the hands of the clock. If I counted slowly, the minute hand would jerk forward to the next fine line on the count of fifty-eight. If I counted slightly faster, the hand would move forward on the count of sixty-five. Or I could count the peacocks on the mantelpiece cover. There were twenty-eight of them. After counting the peacocks, I could have counted the flowers and leaves below them. But in the darkness I could count only my own footsteps. My legs started to hurt again and my head felt heavy. But I wouldn't sit down. Surely it wasn't possible for anyone to fall asleep standing up. It seemed as if my head weighed a ton.

A noise came from outside. It sounded like chee . . . chooo . . .

Some door had opened. A man coughed. From the landing of the house opposite came the tapping of a walking stick. The first light of dawn could be seen. Babu Mangat Ram went for a walk on the dot of 4 a.m. The water tap in the alley began to splutter. Some pale rays of sunlight appeared through the skylight. A feeling of happiness flooded through my whole body. The night was over. Twenty-six days had passed. This time, if I could go the whole month, I wouldn't consider myself such a degenerate. Voices could be heard coming one after another from all the houses in our neighbourhood. These voices extended their help to me. 'Now, don't despair. We won't let you fall asleep. You won't have a wet dream today.'

I went quietly out of the office, and went and lay down on my bed. Everyone was still asleep. A little while later, Father turned over and got up. He said, 'Wake up, son, wake up! Get up and have a bath. Get up! It's four o'clock.'

~

I was standing outside the dispensary. Someone standing in the courtyard of the Arya Samaj was shouting in a very loud voice. 'I'll see to each one of you! I'll have it out with each one of you! I'll make you all answer for this! It's not just anybody you're dealing with here. It's Atmadarshi. I...'

Clad in a long-necked coat and a turban, this person threw his head back and, without directly addressing anyone, as if he were talking to thin air, went on shouting, 'I'll demand an explanation from all of you! It's nine o'clock and the dispensary door hasn't been opened. It's nine o'clock and neither the vaidya nor his compounder is here!'

I caught a glimpse of a yellow dupatta behind the parapet on the top floor. Devaki was standing right up against the parapet.

'I'll make you all answer for this! It's Atmadarshi you have to deal with. This is an outrage. You started a wrestling club. Now it is closed. You were running a seminary, now, out of twenty-five celibates there are only thirteen left, and nobody seems to show any concern. You've opened a dispensary and the doctor goes on sleeping till as late as nine o'clock. The Arya Samaj's money is being wasted . . .'

The courtyard was deserted. Who on earth was this man going on berating?

He still had his head thrown back and, every now and then, he would thump the stick he was holding on the ground. Heaven knows how long he had been standing in that same place. 'The members are having the wool pulled over their eyes. I've been watching everything. You can't hide anything from Atmadarshi. I'll make you all answer for this, I'll ask for explanations from every single one of you. The dispensary employee is being used for housework. I'll see that it all comes out, each and every bit of it . . .'

Atmadarshi's throat was beginning to give out, but, looking neither to the right nor to the left, he stood in the same place with his head thrown back and went on shouting. Devaki was still glued to the parapet behind the window.

I came away from the gate and stepped into the street. I had come to get some medicine from Tulsi for nocturnal emissions, but it didn't seem right to stay there. Even when I reached the crossroads, I could still hear Atmadarshi's voice. I started wandering aimlessly through the streets. For some months now I had started feeling extremely solitary. I would sit apart, wrapped up in my own thoughts. I looked at the face of every passing boy and tried to guess whether he had wet dreams or not. It was as if I were being eaten away by something deep inside me. If a friend of Father's came along, I would turn my head away, because I knew that he would stop and say how thin I had become. And he would know from my face what the matter with me was. Then he would start comparing me with my brother. He was the saint and I was the sinner . . .

Walking along, I reached the tonga stand, where there stood the big town church. Outside the church precincts, a large white strip of cloth had been suspended between two trees. On it was written: 'Unhappy people of the world, repose your faith in Me and I will give you solace.'

I stood reading this and thinking that perhaps the senior padre of the church might have some remedy for nocturnal emissions.

'Hey! What are you doing standing here?' said a voice from behind me. I swung around and found it was Kuldip. He had ridden up on a shiny cycle and stopped behind me. He was sitting well poised on the saddle with one foot on the ground. It was as if, just by seeing him, my distress had been reduced by half. It was many days since I had had anybody to talk to.

'Come on, let's go to the cinema,' he said.

Just listening to him, I began to vacillate.

'No, I've got some work to do,' I said, although I didn't want to wander around in the streets all alone.

'Come on, chum, I've got two tickets. Madan didn't come.'

The cinema was right opposite. He didn't give me a chance to hesitate. In a matter of minutes we were inside the darkened hall, looking for our seats. They were showing *Shirin Farhad*.

My eyes were fixed on the screen. But once inside the hall, I started having regrets. I shouldn't have come here. It was clearly written in *Drops of Nectar* that any boy who had wet dreams shouldn't go to the cinema. But my brother went to the cinema. So did all his friends. Farhad, seated on a rock, was pounding a stone and singing throughout. The screen was very brightly illuminated. We had arrived late and a large part of the film had already been shown.

Suddenly, the lights went up in the hall and sellers of paan and cigarettes came inside, calling their wares.

'I'm going,' I said, getting up.

'Now, where are you going? It's going to be a very good programme.'

Kuldip caught hold of my hand and made me sit down.

'There's going to be a great programme just now, one you've never seen the like of before.'

'What are they going to put on?'

'There's going to be live dancing. An Iranian girl is going to dance. Don't get up now!'

I tried once more to get up, but my head began to pound with curiosity and longing. A black curtain was pulled across the screen and the hall was plunged into darkness. Breathing hard, I fixed my eyes on the stage. Kuldip was still holding on to my hand.

Suddenly, a beam of red light fell on the stage from the right, and we could see a girl standing in the circle it made. It seemed as if it was the red rays of light that had brought her on to the stage. She had a tambourine in her hand and her long golden hair swung about over her shoulders. It was an unearthly scene. The girl was wearing a pleated skirt down to her knees. My heart was still pounding, but it seemed as if I had arrived in some different world.

The girl had one hand on her waist and the other, holding the round tambourine, curved up to her shoulder. She was standing at a slight angle to the audience and kept smiling in their direction.

Suddenly, she tossed her head, stamped her feet on the floor and started dancing to the sound of the tambourine. In the background, somewhere behind the dark curtain, a musical instrument started playing. The circle made by the spotlight followed the girl everywhere.

The spotlight colour changed to green. It seemed even more alluring than before. Sometimes she tapped the tambourine against her right knee, and at other times she played it high above her head. Sometimes she danced in circles with expressive gestures and quick movements of the feet. At such times, her pleated skirt rose to her knees so that her calves showed. Is this what angels looked like?

Suddenly, I started having pangs of conscience. Here I was with my eyes popping, staring at a woman's face when it clearly said in *Drops of Nectar* . . . To take my eyes off her, I started looking downwards, but my eyes were drawn back to the stage. Never before had I had to deal with such a

difficult situation. I had never seen such a beautiful woman
before. Kuldip still had a good grip of me.

With a last rattle of the tambourine, the dance came to
an end. The hall resounded with applause. People started
shouting, 'Encore, encore!' The girl came forward and
bowed to the audience. Her gleaming golden hair fell in
waves over her forehead and shoulders. Some people threw
money on to the stage.

Putting her hand on her heart, the girl thanked the
audience. Then, smiling, she put her right hand on her
bright red lips, and blew kisses to them. The hall was
again in an uproar of shouting and applause. Suddenly,
she disappeared from view. 'She'll come back,' said a man
sitting in front of us.

'No, she won't,' replied the man sitting next to him.

My heart was thumping exactly as before. I was longing
for her to come back on to the stage once more. At the
same time, in my heart of hearts, I was reproaching myself,
and I wanted to get up and leave.

Then they started showing the film all over again.
Farhad was pounding a stone and singing. Coming out of
the cinema, I was in the most searing state of anguish, at
the centre of which, the exceedingly beautiful features of
the dancing girl started floating before my eyes. It seemed
as if she were going on dancing—in ecstasy—in the midst
of those flames of anguish.

My forehead started burning. After leaving the theatre
we went part of the way on Kuldip's cycle, then, just as we
reached the slope of Naya Mohalla, we started walking.

On a sudden, inexplicable impulse, I pushed Kuldip into a darkish alley where there were a few broken-down houses and one or two shops at the end.

'Why have we come here?' he asked.

'Tell me one thing—and be quite truthful. Do you get wet dreams?'

He looked at me and laughed. 'Do you?'

'I am asking you,' I said in a very serious tone.

Getting him to admit that he too had wet dreams was giving me a special sort of satisfaction.

'Yes, I do—now and then.'

'You see? I knew you got them. You've been hiding this from me. After how many days does it happen?'

'I don't know. Just now and then.'

'My dear friend, you're lying!' I snapped, and pushed him farther into the dark alley. He became rather alarmed. I wanted to hear from his own lips that he had more wet dreams than I had. So that I could give him advice. So that I could get him on to the right path.

'Tell me truthfully, how many days elapse between your wet dreams. I won't tell anybody.'

'It happens once or so every month or two.'

'Don't you count the days?'

'Do you?' he asked, laughing.

'I am asking you.'

'I don't count them.'

Up to that point, my gravity had had no effect on him. Getting impatient, I said, 'You're going on laughing, but you don't know what a precious thing semen is. That is why it is called drops of nectar. It takes 400 drops of blood to make one drop of semen, and it gets deposited in the backbone. If you get wet dreams, it weakens your spine. Your whole body becomes weak.'

It seemed to me that my knowledge was beginning to have some effect on him. I went on with my advice. 'Some people masturbate. That is very serious. Their member turns blue. Do you masturbate?'

'Do you?' he asked lightly, as he had done at first.

'I am asking you. If you tell me the truth, I'll help you. I know some ways of stopping wet dreams. If you tell me the truth, your spine will stay straight. And your complexion won't be pale the way it is now.'

Kuldip looked at me in silence. My words were beginning to have some effect. His attitude was also turning serious. I continued, 'You shouldn't ride a cycle. And you should take a cold bath at night. You should chew your food thoroughly before you swallow it.'

His lips were beginning to twist again. Perhaps he was going to smile again.

'Tell me truthfully. Do you masturbate?'

'Do you?'

'I am asking you. I never masturbate. I never even so much as touch that part of me. Yours will turn blue. I'm sure you understand. Tell me the truth. I won't tell anybody.' My voice was getting louder. Even now he was looking at me in quite an unconcerned way.

'Your member must have turned blue by this time. Has it or hasn't it?'

This time he started laughing. 'Mine is blackish. You want to see? Shall I show you?'

And shaking off my arm, he started moving out of the dark alley.

'Get along with you now! I'm getting late! You crazy loon . . . counting the days between one wet dream and the next, indeed!' And mounting his cycle, he made for the mouth of the alley.

I walked along the very edge of the road with my head lowered. Kuldip too had wet dreams. He said it happened once or twice every month or two. But he didn't worry about it. He kept no count of the days. All of a sudden, the moon-like features of the dancer started floating in front of my eyes. I gave my head a good shake. But there she was again. I shook my head over and over again the way horses toss their heads to rid themselves of buzzing flies, but to no avail. That face came before my eyes again, sometimes laughing, sometimes beckoning with a smile, at other times, laughing and blowing kisses to the audience. My head started getting heavy again. Shaking my head like a madman, I went off homewards.

§

The plumes on the horse's head waved in the breeze. The tonga was going at a fast pace from the railway station to the house. The Lahore tongas were decrepit and slow-moving. Lahore horses had been tired for centuries. The horses of my home town went like the wind. The tonga had such a broad seat that you could sit with your legs stretched out. You could go for miles and miles without a single jolt.

I was coming back home after many years. I went on looking eagerly at the streets and houses of my town. It had changed a lot. The railway bridge which used to look gigantic had now started looking quite ordinary. And it was as if the streets had become smaller. Now they didn't look so long or so wide. The afternoon sun was just as bright and welcoming as it used to be before.

The tonga driver, Murtaza, was an old resident of my neighbourhood, the same fellow who used to sing love songs, and to whose voice we had to close our ears. Now Murtaza had a very long moustache, and he was wearing a coachman's khaki turban.

'We don't live in your neighbourhood,' he said. 'We've gone away to the town council locality.'

Hearing this was something of a blow.

Turning the corner, we came into our neighbourhood which seemed smaller.

In place of the coachmen's quarters, in front of which four or five horses always used to be tethered, there now stood a tall building.

'It belongs to Gormang Amjad Ali. He made a lot of money in the army, providing camels. And he brought back sackfuls of currency notes on the backs of those very camels,' said Murtaza.

'Where is Baba Noora?'

'Baba Noora is dead.'

Bostan, the blacksmith, was standing in front of his workshop, clipping a horse's coat with an electric shearer.

The grr-grr of the machine could be heard from quite far away. Electric light poles had been erected in the town streets.

Maulvi Ishaq came out of his house and started walking along the middle of the street. He would, of course, be going to say the fourth prayer of the day. The shop of Attar Singh, the sweetmeat seller, had gone and in its place stood a double-storeyed building with blue chhajjas. The huge rosewood tree, which was right next to his shop, had been cut down.

Mother opened the door. My heart missed a beat. What was wrong with her lips? Mother had become old. The flesh of her face was beginning to sag. And there wasn't a single tooth left in her mouth. Mother made no attempt to hide her lips.

'What has happened to you, Mother?'

'I had my teeth extracted.'

Father was, as usual, sitting in his office and typing out letters with one finger. He got up and clasped me to his chest. I recognized the smell of his body which had never changed over the years.

'Give him some nice hot milk,' he said to Mother, stroking my back. 'It's been a tiring journey for him.' Father's hair was completely white. But, in his moustache, there were only a few white hairs here and there. Father was looking very handsome.

'Where's my brother?' I asked impatiently.

'He'll be coming. We've rented an office in the shopping centre. That's where your brother goes.'

I came out of the office and took a walk around the house. The house too was looking very small. The pole of the lean-to outside the kitchen—the one we used to hold on to for swinging—was now only a little higher than my head. On the cupboard built into the wall, there were still the yellow chalk lines drawn by my little sister as a small child. Her name too was written there: Vimla. One side of the door was open, as if she had forgotten to close it before going away. Over the fireplace, there was still the wood-framed mirror in which I used to look twenty times every day to see whether my complexion had taken on a healthier look or not. A kind of silence had fallen on the whole house. It was as if a fine layer of dust had settled everywhere—like an ageing process.

The house at the rear had been purchased and attached to the house. One of the new rooms was chock-full of books. It also had three full-sized, built-in cupboards, each of which was filled with English books. In two of the rooms there were carpets.

'Your brother keeps having changes made,' said Mother, following me about everywhere. 'He's very enthusiastic. But your father never was and still isn't. Day and night he sits tap-tapping at his typewriter.'

My heart sank when I looked at Mother's pinched-in face.

Walking around, we arrived back at the office.

'Give him some nice warm milk. The journey has tired him,' said Father once again to Mother.

'The servant hasn't come back yet. I'll heat it up myself.'

'Where on earth is Tulsi? Just tell Tulsi to heat the milk.'

The mention of Tulsi's name surprised me. Mother said, 'Look, my dear, how many times have I told you that Tulsi isn't our servant? Why should we get work done by him?'

'Tulsi's here?' I asked Mother.

'Yes, son, he's doing tailoring work, and he comes here to sleep at night. Today he is stitching clothes, sitting in the small mezzanine room above the garage. Your father still has work done by him, but I say it's not right.'

'You've encouraged him to have too high an opinion of himself. If he warms a glass of milk, will it wear out his hands? Besides, what does he mean by staying here? Have we opened a hostelry?'

'Has he left the dispensary?' I asked.

'Oh, a long time ago! Those people quarrelled among themselves, but it was Tulsi who suffered. After that, he tried his hand at a lot of different things. He even went to his village and worked as a hakim.'

In the meantime, Father had kept looking out of the window the way he always used to do. Suddenly, he turned and said, 'Now tell him he should look for a place to live! Send him packing.'

'My dear, let him stay for a couple of days. He hasn't got a job. When he finds one, he'll go away on his own.' Then turning to me, Mother said, 'May God bless your brother. He took Vidya's old sewing machine and gave it to him. In his place, I wouldn't have been all that bold. Now he stitches different kinds of garments.'

'That man is useless, he'll never amount to anything,' said Father. 'He's thick-headed.' Looking at me with great affection, he said, 'You have come back looking not particularly fit. You don't get home-cooked food there, do you?' As he went on looking at me, his whole face brightened.

'Are you studying Sanskrit? You should definitely study it. Persian too is a very good language. *Gulistan* and *Bostan* are very good books.' After muttering something very quietly, he said, 'A Persian writer once said, "If you have to take a handful of earth from a pile of earth, let it be from a big pile." Wasn't that apt?' Looking out of the window, he hummed some couplets for a while, then turning around, he said to Mother, 'Give him some hot milk to drink. He's tired after his journey.'

It didn't take long for quarrels to start between Father and Mother. If Father cut Mother short, she wrinkled her nose and turned away. If Mother cut Father short, Father grumbled, tossed his head and started muttering.

'Isn't tea made at home?' I asked. 'We drink tea there.'

'Why do you have to drink tea?' asked Father reprovingly. 'Grown-up lads shouldn't drink tea. Give him milk.'

'Tea is made in every home now, my dear. What is wrong with making it in our house? Why do you stick your oar into everything?'

'All right, do as you please,' said Father, shaking his head. 'Why do you ask me?'

I went upstairs along with Mother. Mother put a pan of water on the fire and started looking for the tea leaves. I got the cups out of an old cupboard with wire-netting doors. There was a complete set of white cups. My brother must have bought them. Otherwise, there used to be sample cups, not one of which matched another.

Mother couldn't find the tea leaves. She had looked behind all the containers ranged above the fire.

'You can never find anything in this house,' said Mother, muttering as she had always done before. But her voice was rather weary, perhaps because of having had her teeth pulled out. And she had also become fatter.

After searching for some time, Mother went to the balustrade and called, 'Baldev's father, has Sudama come back yet or not?'

'No. What's the matter?'

'I can't find the tea leaves. If he had been here, he could have brought some from the shop.'

'I'll go and get them, Mother,' I said, going to the balustrade.

Father had come out into the courtyard downstairs. Seeing me, he said, 'I'll give you tea. Come downstairs and take this box of tea.'

'Go and fetch it, son,' said Mother. 'Now your Father has gone into the tea business too. He sells tea to his traders from Kabul.'

I ran downstairs. Father gave me a flattish white tin box, of a kind I had never seen before, neither in our own town nor in Lahore. I took it and went upstairs. I banged it repeatedly on the floor to open it.

The leaves were put into boiling water, but they didn't give out any colour. More leaves were added, but still no colour appeared.

'Can you hear me, Baldev's father?' said Mother, going to the balustrade. 'What kind of tea is this you've sent up? It doesn't give any colour.'

Father's voice came from downstairs, 'It's Shanghai tea. It's the very best kind of tea. You won't get tea like this in any of the shops.'

'But why doesn't it give out any colour?'

'But it does. Why wouldn't it?'

'Come and see it. I've already put in a handful of tea leaves, but even then they don't give any colour.'

'How is that possible? I'm coming.'

Father's heavy tread could be heard on the stairs. Now he climbed the stairs very slowly.

'Here, let me see it.' Father looked at the pan of boiling water, then, putting in some tea leaves, asked Mother to put it on the fire.

'It will become bitter, my dear. Nobody makes tea that way.'

'I'm not going to have this tea,' I said, looking at the light yellow colour of the water. 'What kind of tea is this that doesn't have any colour?'

'Are you interested in the tea, or its colour? It's such excellent tea—from Shanghai.'

'I'm not going to drink it.'

'Anyway, young lads shouldn't drink tea,' said Father gently.

The new servant, Sudama, came upstairs. He was a thin, elderly man, with several days' stubble on his chin. He was so splay-footed that his feet seemed to point east and west when he walked. He looked like someone who had run away from a lunatic asylum.

He put a few tea leaves into his mouth, chewed them and rolled his eyes. Then he glanced at the boiling water.

'This is green tea—from green tea leaves. We people don't drink this. It's the Pathans who drink it.'

'If you people drink it, what harm will it do you?' said Father with annoyance.

'I'm not having this tea,' I said softly.

'All right, if you don't want to, don't drink it. Here, give me that box of tea. You people aren't worthy of being given superior tea to drink.' And taking the box of tea, Father started off down the stairs.

Sudama went off to fetch tea from the shops. I went into Father's office and sat down there. Father was becoming somewhat stooped. He also bent lower to be able to see the keyboard of the typewriter.

My gaze turned towards the door. Tulsi was standing on the threshold. It took him a moment to recognize me. Then he joined his hands and displayed his very small teeth and very red gums.

'Tulsi!' I said, getting up and going over to him. He bent down and touched my knees.

'What are you doing?' I said, putting aside his hand. Tulsi again joined his hands. I had become much taller than him. He was still as short as he used to be. His eyes were sunken, and almost all the radiance had gone from his face. He had not had a shave for a long time. Tulsi was leaning with his shoulder against the doorpost just as he used to do years ago.

I saw that we had nothing to say to each other. We were both feeling embarrassed. We went to one side of the courtyard.

'Are you quite well and happy?' Standing with his hands joined, he peered at me as if his eyesight had become weak.

'Is our sister-in-law, your wife, quite well? Is she here or in the village?' I asked.

He was silent for a moment, then he said, 'Devaki is dead. She died in childbirth. She died when she had our second child.' Tulsi was still peering at me with his sunken eyes. His chin began to tremble. He wiped his eyes with the end of his turban. I put my hand on his shoulder. He started sobbing convulsively. My tongue felt paralysed. I couldn't get out a single word.

'Where are your children?' I finally asked, softly.

'They're both in the village. They're with my brother, Amichand.'

Then wiping his eyes again with the end of his turban, he looked at me with great affection. 'The boy is now quite big, he's seven years of age. The girl is still quite small.'

'What have you called them?'

He smiled slightly. 'The boy's name is Ved, the girl's is Shanti!' Tulsi had given them traditional Arya Samaj names.

'Mother said you were now doing tailoring jobs.'

'That's right. The dispensary people dismissed me, so I worked for a while with Pandit Sitaram. But all I did there was grind medicines. There actually wasn't much work. And he didn't teach me anything.'

'How does tailoring suit you?'

Tulsi was silent. Then he said, 'Now I stitch shirts and pyjamas. Baldev got me a place to sit on the landing of a shop. But, you see, I hadn't learnt tailoring.' Then he came close and whispered in my ear, 'If I say anything to Father, he gets angry. So please ask him to give me a peon's job in his bank. He will do it, of course, but if you ask, he'll do it quicker.'

Tulsi talked with the confidence of someone who belonged in the family, and who knew how to get Father to agree to his request.

'Come here, Tulsi, come here a minute.' It was Father's voice. 'Here, take these letters and run straight to the town post office with them. If the mail has already been cleared, don't even consider coming back home. Go straight to the railway station. Here, take them.'

Tulsi took the letters, put on his shoes, and rushed off just as he used to do.

The sound of somebody talking loudly could be heard coming from the street. The noises were familiar. Two men were quarrelling.

'Let go of him. Are you a father or a butcher?'

That was my brother's voice. I ran across to the office window. My brother wasn't visible in the street, but his voice sounded even louder than before. 'What's it to me? He's your son. And when he grows up he won't even want to see your face.'

Father came and stood in the middle of the office. Mother, feeling very disturbed, came downstairs.

'Like father, like son. God knows with whom he's got involved.'

My brother was holding a little boy in his arms, and a short bearded man in a Turkish cap was glaring at him.

Maulvi Ishaq's son and his cousin came out of the opposite house.

'What Babu says is right. Why are you beating an innocent child?'

The bearded man kept staring in a bemused manner at my brother. Then he gently held his child's hand and took him from my brother. 'I won't beat him, my friend, but I want the little rascal to study!'

And making the boy walk along with him, he left the alley.

My brother embraced me. He had shaved off his moustache and was wearing a coat and trousers.

'Why didn't you write? I'd have come to the railway station.'

My brother exuded confidence. 'We beat Abinashi Ram hollow in no uncertain manner. He won't forget this defeat in a hurry.'

'Who is Abinashi Ram?'

It turned out there were two parties in the College Management Committee. Abinashi Ram was the head of one of them. There had recently been a vote. That is what my brother was alluding to.

'Just yesterday, he was voted out. Before the vote we went on the quiet from house to house and collected subscriptions from all those who hadn't paid up, and they all landed up to vote. You should have seen Abinashi Ram's face.'

I wanted to ask him about old friends.

'How's Ramesh?'

'He's just fine. I got his engagement broken off.'

'He'd got engaged?'

'They had forced him to get engaged to somebody against his will. His uncle had gone and given his word to some family. Ramesh didn't want to marry into that family, but he didn't dare say so.'

'So what did you do?'

'There's a man in their community who was actively involved in it. You must know him. Mansa Ram. He used to run a general store in Rajah Bazaar. I wrote an anonymous letter to him, saying that the marriage shouldn't take place, because the boy was impotent, and asked what point there would be in ruining the girl's life.'

'Then what happened?'

'But, you know, he found out who had written the letter. I had sent it through our munshi, and he recognized him. The next day he came and complained to Father.

He was raging mad, but we stood firm. Now he won't be getting married to that girl. Ramesh is very happy.'

Listening to the things my brother told me, this sleepy town came to life again in my imagination. It was becoming lively and engaging. A ripple of life was passing through its dreary, shady streets.

'Rest, if you're feeling tired. In the morning I'll take you to the pool. We'll go swimming there.'

'But there isn't a pool here. What pool is this?'

'We looked around and found one. If you go about two miles beyond Tapovan, you find the water of the stream is very clear. There's a spot there where a dried-up tree has fallen across the stream. This has made the water deeper and the banks are really high. Ramesh really enjoys jumping into it holding his nose. He doesn't know how to dive. He jumps straight in. You'll enjoy it.'

'Will Ramesh be going too?'

'No, his foot got hurt.'

My brother recalled the incident. 'A very odd thing happened,' he said, sounding somewhat embarrassed. 'One day, Ramesh and I were standing together a little way off from the pool. We were stark naked. We bathe in the nude there because the place is deserted. In the meantime, from somewhere behind us, a lady came strolling along. God knows how she had got there. We both ran and jumped into the water, but Ramesh's foot got injured.'

'Do you like commerce?' I asked my brother.

'No, I'm not going to stay in business. But at present, we are trying to promote Horrock's long cloth.'

I didn't understand this. Seeing my confusion, my brother started explaining. 'Look, you know what cotton fabric is, don't you? The material of which they make salwars and pyjamas. This cotton sells well. You must have heard of Key Brand long cloth and 57 Brand long cloth. These are the popular brands. Chanan Shah Bajaj has the agency for 57 Brand long cloth.'

'What does "Horrock" mean?'

'Horrock is a brand name. Do you know what I did? I sent Ramesh to a few shops. He would go to a shop and ask, "Have you got Horrock's long cloth?" Then he would go to another shop and ask them the same question. A few days later, I got hold of some other friends and sent them too. That way, the shopkeepers got to know the brand name of the cloth. But, you know, they still aren't giving us any orders. We hope we'll gradually start getting them.'

'Is Tulsi staying in the house?'

'Oh yes. Hasn't he met you?'

'Yes, he has.'

'You know, he doesn't know anything about stitching clothes. Yesterday somebody beat him up in the market. He makes clothes any old way, the way Mother used to. So somebody got hold of him and beat him up . . . All right now. Tell us what you have been doing. Have you been playing a lot of hockey? How did your exams go? Listen! Let's go to Murree on cycle. You and I. It would be great fun.'

'That's forty miles away. And it's in the hills.'

'That's no distance at all. We'll go on our cycles as far as Chattar. Then we'll climb into some truck. And we'll come back on our cycles. Come on, let's go. We'll really enjoy it. We've got one cycle at home and we'll get another one from Ramesh. Come on, we'll go and get it, it's still early. All right, you relax, I'll go and get it.'

And my brother left the house to go and get Ramesh's cycle.

ॐ

Where does the real course of one's life actually begin? At what turning point does one leave one's boyhood behind and start on manhood? Who can say that, before that point, everything was clouded and unclear and without significance, but that everything ahead of it will be clear and meaningful? Isn't manhood as hazy as childhood? And doesn't that haziness go on right to the end of one's life?

I became deeply involved in business affairs. In the jumble of images which surge up before my eyes, I was sitting with a bank clerk, who was telling me how a cash book was to be kept. He was a fair-skinned youth and, although younger than I was, he did his work with great efficiency. Peons delivered D.O.s and within minutes he made the entries in the cash book. Seconds after receiving papers, he marked them in red ink. I couldn't understand a thing. Father had said, 'You must learn bank work. That will be a great advantage to you in business.' The clerk behaved very respectfully to me, because I was not an employee there.

I heard a voice coming from behind me. 'I don't tell lies. I never tell lies.'

I recognized the voice. It was gruff and deep. I turned slightly and saw that it was Tulsi. But then I turned back because, although I knew he was working here, I didn't want him to see me.

'You are falsely accusing me of lying, Babu. I never tell lies.'

The voice got louder and more strident.

I felt like turning around towards Tulsi and asking him what the matter was, but I bent my head over the table and sat quite still. However, I kept listening.

'Hey, Tulsi Ram!' It was some clerk calling him. Then I heard a chair scraping on the floor and the sound of rapid footsteps.

'What are you doing? Stop him! What kind of man is this we've got here?'

I couldn't stop myself from turning my head and looking. Tulsi had his back to me, so he couldn't see me. With his face averted, Tulsi Ram had lowered his head over his arm. This position was not new to me. I had seen this years before. And yet my skin broke out in gooseflesh. Tulsi Ram had pulled up his sleeve and had sunk his teeth into his arm. The clerk who had just got up from his chair tried to get him to stop, but Tulsi wouldn't let go of his own arm. He was wearing spectacles which were tied around his ears with thread.

'He'll really injure his arm. Get him to stop. Go and get the manager.'

'Tulsi, let go! Let go, Tulsi! I didn't say anything to you.'

Tulsi finally let go of his arm. There was blood on his lips. His skin remained flushed and deep red. He didn't look across at me. He didn't look across at anybody. Stifling his sobs, he went outside to the teller's railing. Then, sitting down on the floor with his head between his knees, he started weeping. His shoulders kept shaking in his sweat-soaked khaki shirt. I was still sitting glued to my chair. No, I shouldn't go to Tulsi. That would embarrass him. He would feel upset. He would be made to feel small. The clerk sitting behind me was laughing.

'I didn't say anything to him. All I asked him was whether he had gone to show the client the FIR or not. And he sank his teeth into his arm.'

'He's mad.'

Gradually, the conversation petered out and the sound of the clerks' pens could be heard. Tulsi was still sitting to one side by the teller's railing with his head between his knees.

Somebody called out, 'Tulsi! Come here, Tulsi!'

I raised my head and looked.

'Tulsi, get up. Bring a glass of water,' said the teller, leaning forward and looking through the grille.

Tulsi raised his head.

'Get up and bring a glass of water,' the man said once again. 'Why is your face all swollen? What's the matter with you? Just bestir yourself and put some effort into your work!'

Tulsi quietly got up and went towards the three round earthenware vessels placed against the opposite wall.

'Wash the glass properly,' the teller called out again, then bent over his register once more.

Tulsi took the glass of water over to the teller. I again bowed my head and put my arm in front of my face so that he wouldn't recognize me . . .

∽

Outside the kitchen, the family—now quite small—got up from the table, having finished dinner. Now we sat at a dining table and no longer ate in the kitchen. At that time, my sister Vidya had come with her two children. They would be staying for a few days. Her boy was almost five and extremely active. He ran around the table, saying, 'Catch me! Catch me!' Sometimes, he sat beneath the table and said, 'Look for me, where am I?' Father had engaged the same Pandit for him who had taught us Hindi and Sanskrit. Father, on his own, helped him to learn the gayatri mantra by heart.

But there was tension in the house. For many days there had been a heaviness in the atmosphere. I was apprehensive. Who could tell what was going to happen? Who could tell? Mother was talking in an undertone to my sister outside the kitchen. This whispering had been going on at home for quite some time now. Sometimes, it would be Father and Mother sitting by themselves and talking in low tones, at other times, it would be Mother and my brother, or my brother and Father.

My brother and Father went straight into the sitting room. An argument had again started between them. For many days now, Father had been trying to convince my brother with one argument or another. But he wouldn't give in. The tension was over only one thing. My brother wanted to get out of business, leave home and go away to some other town. Father wanted to hold him back.

Father called me and said, 'Go and fetch the big black ledger from downstairs.'

'Father, I know what's written in it. I haven't forgotten anything,' said my brother irritably.

I went and fetched it.

Father opened the ledger and said to me, 'Read out what's written there.'

'I know all this, Father, and it doesn't make any difference,' said my brother, turning away.

Standing behind the ledger, I read out from it, with Father following each line with one finger.

'Harrison & Crossfield, March, 1550 rupees; April, 1200 rupees; May, 600 rupees; June 1200 rupees . . .'

'And that's the commission from just one firm,' said Father, turning to another page of the ledger.

I read out, 'Jacob Barnes & Sons, April, 405 rupees; May, 130 rupees . . .'

'There's no point in it, Father. I know all this,' said my brother, cutting him short.

'But does business have any limit? If you don't want to deal in cloth and tea, deal in something else. I have thirty years' standing in commerce. I'll write letters to different places and get you other agencies. What are you apprehensive about?'

'It's not that I'm apprehensive about anything. I just don't like business and I don't want to be in it.'

'What objection do you have to it?' asked Father, laughing.

Father put his arguments in a number of different ways, sometimes forcefully, sometimes cajolingly.

'I've no objection to it, but my heart is not in business.'

'If you don't want to operate from here, open an office in some other town.'

My brother shook his head in silence.

'In business, the greater the efforts you make, the further you go. I was all alone, I was poor and there was nobody to help me. But you . . . you have everything!'

I knew the argument would gradually go from bad to worse. Why did these two have to keep going over the same thing?

'There are some who yearn for mothers and there are others who yearn for stepmothers,' said Father.

I had never fully understood this saying of Father's, but he was fond of repeating it.

'You have to proceed in life with the greatest forethought. I'm saying this for your own good. What will you get out of leaving home and being severely knocked about? I've taken plenty of knocks myself. The wise man is one who learns from others' experience.'

'I'm not going into trade and I'm leaving home.'

'When you leave home, what will you do? You should at least tell us.'

'I don't know myself what I'm going to do. But I won't stay here.'

'Why do you distress yourself and also cause me distress? You should give some thought to what you are saying,' said Father, becoming annoyed.

My brother remained obdurate.

Suddenly Father became very upset and, taking off his turban, he bowed his white head before my brother. 'Have some regard for these white hairs. Now I'm getting old and how much longer am I going to work? Have some pity on me.'

My heart missed a beat and I started feeling angry at my brother's obstinacy. I looked up at my brother. He sat there unmoved.

'Everyone has to grow old one day, Father. One day I too will grow old.'

I began to think my brother was heartless. Did he really have no pity in his heart?

'Father, I'm not running away from home. I'm just getting out of business. I'll do some other kind of work. You yourself left service to start up in business.'

'What was my status then? I was being paid just twenty-five rupees a month as a clerk.'

Then Father held out both his hands before my brother. Father had eczema in both hands. It had been troubling him for many years.

'Have you no feeling left? You can't even see this?' said Father, his voice breaking with emotion.

Mother came into the room. 'Look, my dear, whatever is written in the child's destiny, is bound to happen. Why are you stopping him? When fledglings grow wings, do they stay on in the nest? They don't. They fly up and away.'

Father interrupted her. 'Why do you interfere?'

'Look, my dear, I am stupid and illiterate and you people are clever and wise. But it's all plain and simple. The child doesn't want to do business, so why are you forcing him into it? You have done whatever your duty was. You gave him a good education and made him fit to stand on his own two legs. Now whatever lies ahead of him is a matter of his own luck in life.'

Father stared at the floor, muttering. Mother went on talking. 'Beyond that, it's up to him. For better or for worse, who are we to interfere? You are quite pointlessly torturing yourself. It doesn't achieve anything.'

'Is my nose to be stuck to the grindstone all my life?' asked Father suddenly, in a loud voice. 'I'm not able to work anymore. If he doesn't want to do it, let him not. An established business will go to the dogs.'

'Now why do you get worried, my dear, what good does that do? The child will go, he won't let you stop him. Send him off in a happy frame of mind. How I long for everything in this house to go peacefully and smoothly! We are a small family. After all, we have just two sons. But no!'

And suddenly Mother's eyes were filled with tears, and she started wiping them with the end of her dupatta.

Earlier, Mother never used to cry, but now tears came very quickly to her eyes. On such occasions, she must remember her daughters, who went away, one after the other. But she never allowed their names to come to her lips . . .

ॐ

Downstairs, in the room with all the books, my brother and I were half-reclining on the carpet.

My brother had written on a sheet of paper: 'On all goods coming from abroad, the price is fixed by adding freight and insurance to all the initial costs. They call this C.I.F. and C.I. But suppose the goods are lying in Bombay. And you buy them from there. The seller will quote the Bombay F.O.R. price, which means that he will deliver the goods to the railway station, then from there on you will pay for rail transport and all other expenses . . .'

My brother was teaching me the intricacies of business. That night, he was going to Lahore. What he was going to do there was not at all clear even to himself. Father took me aside. I don't know how many times he had told me to ask my brother what he was going to do in Lahore. But I couldn't tell him anything. He talked of bringing out a newspaper, acting in plays, and writing. All kinds of things kept occurring to him.

I could hear Father's voice from the courtyard. That day, he repeatedly came out of the office. He called out to

Mother, 'Baldev's mother, please make some sweet *pinni*s to send along with him.'

'My dear, what are you thinking of? His train leaves at seven. Am I supposed to start making pinnis now? Just think if this is the right time.'

'Have I said anything wrong? Pinnis made with pure ghee are very good. He'll be happy to have them with him.'

'Now look, my dear . . .' Mother started talking again.

But behind her stood my sister who pulled at her dupatta just as she used to do years ago. She whispered to her, 'Mother, just say you'll make them. What's the point of arguing? He's not going to open up Baldev's luggage to see whether the pinnis have been put in or not.'

'All right, if I can make them, I will.'

Father was standing in the doorway of our room. He had a cheque in his hand. 'Here, take this, Baldev. And have it deposited directly in the bank. I'll also write to the bank manager. Don't be over-thrifty. There's always more expense away from home. Don't try to economize too much.'

My brother took the cheque.

Father went away to the office, but within a minute he was back. He had brought a whole bundle of postcards. As had been his wont for many years, he placed them in my brother's hands and said, 'There you are, that's sixteen postcards. Post one every three or four days. I've written the message on all of them. I've left some space below for you to write anything else you yourself might want to.'

I was amazed. Each postcard bore the same sentence: 'Father, I am quite well and happy, please don't worry.' Even his name was written below—Baldev. Father had also written his address on each postcard.

'I know you people. Both you brothers are very lazy about writing letters. But you can do this at least, can't you? Or you won't even do this?'

My brother took the postcards and put them into his pocket.

'Put them into your inside pocket,' said Father.

'They're all right here, Father.'

'No, put them in the inside pocket.'

'All right, I'll put them there.'

'No, do it here in front of me . . . There, that's better.'

I looked out from the inner to the outer courtyard. Tulsi was standing on the threshold. He was carrying a staff and a small bag, and he had a boy of seven or eight beside him.

'Tulsi!' I called out his name, and got up and went over to him. Coming forward, Tulsi put his staff and bundle down on the ground, then touched Father's feet with both hands.

'When did you come from the village, Tulsi?' asked Father. Without waiting for an answer, he went off towards the office.

Tulsi had gone back to his village after losing the job at the bank. He seemed to have come back in a state of distress. The little boy was still standing in the courtyard, looking thoroughly lost. Tulsi stood outside the office, leaning against the jamb of the door with his hands joined. Now, he would join his hands at the slightest pretext.

'Is Mother quite well?'

'Yes, yes, she's quite all right,' said Father, sitting in his chair and repeatedly shaking his right knee from side to side. Whenever Father did this, we took it that something was bothering him. He didn't like Tulsi's having come at this juncture.

'Do you get letters from sister Vidya?'

'Vidya is upstairs. Go and meet her.'

Tulsi had a tired, worn-out look about him. Talking to him, I felt a sense of shame that my brother was going away from home to make his way in life, while Tulsi's career, having come to serious grief years ago, was now over.

Tulsi turned towards the stairs. Mother was coming downstairs. Seeing Tulsi, she stopped. 'Come on then, Tulsi, it's ages since we've seen you.'

Stepping forward, Tulsi touched Mother's feet with both hands.

'Is this your son?'

'Go and touch Mother's feet.'

Ved touched Mother's feet with great alacrity. Mother laughed. 'He is smarter than his father. May God give him a long life!'

Father came out of the office with another letter and called to my brother. 'You've taken care of all your luggage, haven't you, Baldev? Here, take this letter. It's addressed to the president of the Arya Samaj in Lahore. Definitely go and meet him. He will give you all kinds of help.'

'Where is Baldev going?' Tulsi asked me very quietly.

'He's going to Lahore.'

Tulsi's face remained expressionless. Shaking his head and distractedly fingering my coat buttons, he said, 'I've brought Ved along. Please keep him as a servant. Please, young sir, you ask Father. If I ask, he will get angry.'

'What are you doing these days?'

'I will also find some small job here. May Father always look upon me with kindness!'

'Why don't you keep your son with you?'

'If he lives here, he'll get some education. He'll pick up good ideas.'

He'd get an education! It sounded as if Tulsi were speaking ironically.

My sister was standing upstairs at the balustrade. 'My goodness, it's Tulsi!' she said, and came rushing downstairs. 'When did you arrive, Tulsi? It must be ten or twelve years since I've seen you. Is this your son? Does he too wash his hair with lentils the way you used to do?'

And my sister exploded with laughter. Remembering things which had happened many years ago, she began to mimic somebody: 'I have done nothing, Lala, except watch the broken pitcher being thrown.'

All this unrestrained laughter reached Father's ears. He came out of his office.

'Are you people going to let me get on with my work or not? Tulsi, go and sit in the courtyard.'

Tulsi took his son and quietly went to the courtyard. Sitting on the doorstep, for the first time, he looked like someone who didn't belong at all to the household.

Father went back into his office. All along, Mother had been sitting on the couch. Now my sister Vidya also came and sat down beside her.

'Mother, Tulsi has brought his son to get him taken on as a servant,' I said quietly into Mother's ear.

Mother laughed again. 'Can't he find any other house? He goes around everywhere, then lands back here.'

Father heard this. He raised his head and said, 'Don't even think of it. In the first place, he wouldn't ever think of leaving the house again. Every third day, he lands up here. Now, he'll again stick to us like a limpet. Just send him packing. If you people won't tell him, I will.' And he got up as if to do so.

'Look, my dear, on a day like this you shouldn't reprove anyone. You should consider what you're saying. Your son is going away from home. Just give that some thought.'

And Mother, in this new way of hers, wrinkled her nose, shook her hands and looked towards my sister.

'What did I say? All right now, don't talk, let me finish the letter.' And, bowing his head again, he got busy writing the letter. In the meantime, Baldev had also come into the room. Mother and my sister again started talking in whispers. 'I'll take on Tulsi's son,' said my sister. 'He'll take Rajiv out for walks.'

'Take him on! Where's the harm? He's somebody we know.'

And my sister, remembering some old story about Tulsi, started smiling and laughing.

Looking at Baldev, I began to have a lost sort of feeling. Between us, we had made a plan that in the month of December I would go to Lahore and we would stay together for a month, we would go out and about a lot. But in spite of this, something seemed to be breaking apart inside me.

Having finished the letter, Father put it in an envelope and closed it. Tilting his head, he looked at the clock. Mother and my sister were both silent. 'Your chatter has delayed things.' And he started shaking his head with annoyance. 'It would have been better if the letter had gone today.' Then he suddenly got up from his chair and called Tulsi. Tulsi came running. 'Run and post these two letters in the town post office. Hurry up. What are you gaping at me for?'

Inside, sitting on the couch, Mother laughed. Then she wrinkled her nose and shook her hands.

⌁

Moonlight streamed down, just as it had done for years during this month. Lying on the roof, looking at the limitless expanse of stars, I felt specks of stardust had been spread everywhere. Without even wishing to, I looked admiringly at them from the coolness of my bed. If you looked intently at one star, it seemed to be twinkling. Sometimes it looked pink and at other times, green.

From the surrounding houses of the neighbourhood, the sounds of kitchens being cleaned up became audible. In the house to the rear, somebody was feeling thirsty and was pouring water out of an earthenware vessel. Beds were being put out on roofs for people to sleep on. The sounds of bread baskets and curd vessels being brought upstairs could be heard.

From the roof of the third house to the rear came the sounds of an old game being played:

> *We come all flower–bedecked,*
> *In the cool weather, in the cool weather!*
> *Whom have you come for, come for?*
> *In the cool weather!*

Voices were coming from the roof of Ishwar Das's house. My sister Vidya's son Rajiv had gone to play there. Tulsi's son was with him to look after him. I tried to make out Rajiv's voice among those of the other children . . .